The Rule of the Door
and Other
Fanciful Regulations

LLOYD BIGGLE, Jr.

The Rule of the Door and Other Fanciful Regulations

WILDSIDE PRESS
Berkeley Heights, NJ • 1999

WILDSIDE PRESS
P.O. Box 45
Gillette, NJ 07933-0045

THE RULE OF THE DOOR: first published in *Galaxy Science Fiction*, February 1958. Copyright © 1957 by Galaxy Publishing Corporation.

PETTY LARCENY: first published in *Satellite Science Fiction*, August 1958. Copyright © 1958 by Lloyd Biggle, Jr.

ON THE DOTTED LINE: first published in *If Worlds of Science Fiction*, June 1957. Copyright © 1957 by Quinn Publishing Company, Inc.

JUDGEMENT DAY: first published in *Fantastic Universe Science Fiction*, April 1958. Copyright © 1958 by King-Size Publications, Inc.

SECRET WEAPON: first published in *Galaxy Science Fiction*, May 1958, as "Bridle Shower." Copyright © 1958 by Galaxy Publishing Corporation.

THE PERFECT PUNISHMENT: first published in *Worlds of Tomorrow*, March 1965, as "Pariah Planet." Copyright © 1965 by Galaxy Publishing Corporation.

A SLIGHT CASE OF LIMBO: first published in *Analog*, April 1963. Included in THE NINTH ANNUAL OF THE YEAR'S BEST SF, edited by Judith Merril (Simon & Schuster, 1964). Copyright © 1963 by Conde Nast Publications, Inc.

D.F.C.: first published in *If Worlds of Science Fiction*, February 1957, as "Cronus of the D.F.C." Published in *Ellery Queen's Mystery Magazine*, September 1966, as "Department of Future Crime." Copyright © 1956 by Quinn Publishing Company, Inc.

WINGS OF SONG: first published in *The Magazine of Fantasy and Science Fiction*, November 1963. Copyright © 1963 by Mercury Press, Inc.

CONTENTS

INTRODUCTION

Early in his conscious existence man began to wonder.

The small world he inhabited was besieged by massive un-
knowns: the hills on the horizon, the foreboding shapes of
primeval forests, that unutterable mother of mysteries, the sea.
Fearfully he asked himself what lay beyond, and what would
happen to him if he went there—or if whatever was there came
to him.

Eventually he went and did not believe what he found, for
until quite late in his history man's wonderings were far more
puissant than the realities that confronted them; and whenever he surmounted a barrier another lay on the horizon—to
be wondered about.

His awakening consciousness began to probe other barriers:
what lay beyond tomorrow? Or beyond the stars? Or beyond
life?

As with most human endeavors there were men who specialized in wondering and became professionals. Today some of
them write *Science Fiction*.

That term has been examined semantically and found wanting, for it links a word referring to objectivity, systematized
knowledge, factuality, and—ultimately—truth, with one meaning the opposite, something feigned or imagined; but science
devoid of imagination has fostered more false doctrine than
all of the purposeful fictions ever spun. Science Fiction com-
bines man's most venerable literature with his most modern;
his hereditary awe of the unknown and his compulsion to

wonder about it with speculation concerning the fearsome power science has given to him to shape his own destiny—or destroy it.

Primitive man inhabited a terrifying world where even a faint breeze was a question mark and a slash of lightning a stroke of doom. He did not think of his wonderings as Science Fiction, but they were. Man inevitably speculates about the unknown in terms of the known, and the word "science" originally meant "knowledge." *Throughout human history every age has produced a "science fiction" that reflected its own technology and scientific thought.*

Primitive man peopled his wonderings with spirits; the ancient Greeks, with gods. Only to later men were such tales superstitions and myths. Homer's audiences accepted his epics as history, and to a surprising extent they were; but they were also the "science fiction" of that age, the realization of man's wonderings in terms of his understanding of his environment some eight hundred years before Christ.

Several major themes of today's Science Fiction have an un-broken development from man's earliest wonderings, with deep roots in his most ancient folklore and myths. The fantastic journey must have fascinated man long before Ulysses's epic tour of Mediterranean wonders. It still fascinates, whether through the voids of space or the recent *Fantastic Voyage* through a human body. The amazing creatures described in travel stories of the past are in their way quite as remarkable as the fabricated *bug-eyed monsters* that populate remote worlds in today's Science Fiction. Lost, or unknown, or undis-covered tribes, races, civilizations, continents, worlds have occupied man's wonderings since he first projected his imagi-nation beyond the horizon. The archetypal utopia was doubtless dreamed during a period of overpopulation and cave shortages in the Pleistocene, the interplanetary romance is no more modern than the second century A.D., and visitors from outer space have a venerable history. The artificial man, or robot, was already present in myths concerning ancient Crete.

There are significant differences between today's Science Fiction and the "science fiction" of earlier times, and two of them may be seen in the use of the words "science" and "fiction." Changes in science and technology have wrought changes in man's wonderings, and changes in literature have affected the forms in which they are expressed. The gradual emergence of fiction as a respectable literary medium relieved writers of the necessity of presenting speculative literature as true experience (though the practice will certainly endure as long as there is a gullible public susceptible of hoaxing for fun or profit). Man's wonderings were cast in the form of fiction at least as early as Aristophanes, however. A Science Fiction scientifically oriented in the modern sense was not possible before the tremendous scientific and technological advances of the nineteenth century, and because these transformed the human environment within the scope of a man's lifetime and so obviously presaged a continuing, accelerating progress, they made possible new dimensions in wondering. The prophets of other ages sought the future in the stars, or in sacrificial divinations, or in drug-induced dreams; the modern prophet consults technical journals and his slide rule. For the first time in human history it has seemed possible to *calculate* the future.

Finally, today's Science Fiction reflects modern man's widening horizons. Homer's Mediterranean world could encompass the wonderings of two epics; but men went out to Homer's horizons and to the horizons beyond, and the blank spaces on the maps of the Earth were gradually filled in. Even on this shrunken planet there is still room enough in which to wonder, and writers who do so continue to discover unknown worlds: A. Conan Doyle's South American *The Lost World* and James Hilton's Himalayan *Lost Horizon*, to name only two twentieth-century examples. Others have been glimpsed in such unlikely locations as down a rabbit hole, with Alice.

But increasingly man has turned his attention outward and inward. On the one hand the space sciences, and on the other such developing sciences as psychiatry, psychology, and sociology probe today's ultimate barriers: outer space and man himself. In the past three thousand years man has explored a world and discovered two universes—one in the sky and the other in his own mind. Today he wonders; tomorrow, give or take a few millennia, he will know, but long before then he will have sighted new horizons.

To wonder about.

Lloyd Biggle, Jr.
Ypsilanti, March 1967

The Rule of the Door
and Other
Fanciful Regulations

1

THE RULE OF THE DOOR

Professor Skarn Skukarn twisted abruptly on the billowy expanse of his bed and sat up. A glance at the pink-tinted indicator told him that the Time of Sleep was no more than half expired. He stretched himself, indulged in a leisurely yawn, rubbed his eyes.

"Strange," he murmured. "Perhaps it was that *sliff* I had for dinner."

He immediately rejected this idea as an assumption unworthy of a distinguished psychologist and padded softly into his laboratory. His lecture notes lay stacked neatly on his desk. He thumbed through the metallic sheets, mildly surprised that he felt no trace of fatigue. His mind was alert; his ideas flowed with sparkling clarity. For a moment he hesitated, thoughtfully gazing at his notes, and then he slipped into his flowing professorial gown and mounted the incongruously ornate lectern that stood in one corner of the laboratory. Smiling faintly, he pressed a button and waited.

Throughout the length and breadth of the great university city of Kuln, oaths and screams of dismay would be curdling the air as hundreds of students were tumbled from their beds by their tingling wrist bands. They would scramble for their viewers, asking themselves, "What's the old fool up to now?"

The thought pleased him. He was not cruel like some of his colleagues, who took fiendish delight in tormenting their students during the Time of Sleep; but it would be an interesting psychological experiment, he told himself, to see how much knowledge a sleep-fogged mind could absorb. He would deliver one of his more difficult lectures and follow it immediately with an examination.

He waited the minimum time that custom allowed him, and began, "Lecture nine hundred seventy-two. The effect of radiation impulses on motor pathways of the subconscious."

He hesitated. His own wrist band tingled sharply, almost painfully. With a sudden surge of panic he understood what it was that had awakened him. He bounded away, scrambled back to the lectern to announce, "To be continued," pressed the cancellation button, and hurried off to his own viewer.

The Prime Minister's face stared out at him, alarmingly pale, haggard, eyelashes crinkly with fatigue. Skarn could easily guess who it was that had disturbed *his* sleep. The Prime Minister scowled and said enviously, "You are looking well, Skarn."

"Likewise," Skarn murmured politely.

"I am not looking well. I am looking miserable. I'm tired."

"Naturally," Skarn agreed.

"An Imperial Assignment. You will begin at once."

Skarn clucked his tongue ecstatically. Such an honor did not come more than two or three times in the entire span of living, even to a high-ranking professor of the Royal University. "I shall serve with pleasure," he announced. "May I inquire—"

"You may. A patrol ship has discovered another inhabited planet. His Imperial Majesty desires a specimen of the dominant life form for the Royal Collection."

Skarn stirred uneasily, and a bluish flush of irritation tinged the smooth white flesh of his face. "I am no pickler of lizards," he growled.

"That you are not," the Prime Minister acknowledged.

"May I inquire—"

"You may. The dominant life form on the planet is intelligent."

"I still fail to comprehend why a psychologist is required."

"The Rule of the Door applies."

Skarn scratched his bald head thoughtfully and hoped he was not making a fool of himself. "That Rule is unfamiliar to me," he admitted. "May I inquire—"

"You may. The Rule of the Door was propounded by the Great Kom when an Imperial Ancestor of His Imperial Majesty desired a specimen of an intelligent life form."

Skarn bowed deeply at the mention of the venerable psychologist of psychologists. "It is no doubt an excellent Rule."

"It has been canonized, along with the other magnificent Rules propounded by the Great Kom. However, this being only the second time in countless glims that an Imperial Majesty has requested an intelligent specimen, the Rule has not been much used."

"Naturally," Skarn agreed.

"In fact, the Rule is no longer included in the Canon of Rules. Were it not for the superb memory of His Imperial Majesty's Prime Minister, the Rule would not have been followed at this time of crisis."

"You are to be congratulated."

"His Imperial Majesty has already done so."

"The Rule of the Door," Skarn mused. "May I inquire—"

"You may. The content of the Rule has been lost."

"In my most humble opinion, the Rule can then be followed only with extreme difficulty."

"His Imperial Majesty does not minimize the difficulty. It was this problem that caused him to summon such a distinguished psychologist as yourself. At my suggestion, of course. Your task is to rediscover the content of the Rule of the Door, to follow it scrupulously, and to obtain for His Imperial Majesty the desired specimen."

Skarn bowed. "I shall direct all of my unworthy talent to the task."

"Naturally," the Prime Minister said. "You will, of course, be granted an unlimited expense account."

"Naturally. I shall also require unlimited time."

"Naturally."

"I shall also," Skarn said, pausing to cluck his tongue in anticipation, "require Imperial Permission to search the Sacred Archives."

"Naturally. I shall expect your presence at the Imperial Palace immediately."

The viewer darkened. Skarn manipulated the dials, saw the acceptance light flash, and stepped through to the Imperial Palace.

For three full cycles of Sleep and Consciousness Skarn tirelessly prowled through the Sacred Archives, probing pile after pile of metallic sheets until his fingers became clumsy with numbness and his eyes so encrusted with fatigue that he almost leafed past the lost Theorems of Wukim without recognizing them. So exhausted was he when he came upon the legendary Speculations of Kakang that he wept; he could no longer read with comprehension. Not until he finally discovered, in a damp corner, the stack of sheets as tall as himself that were the notebooks of the Great Kom, did he observe a Time of Sleep.

He returned to them refreshed, and duty and curiosity waged a heated contest within him until he effected a deft psychological compromise. He read through the notebooks with reverent care, but only until he found the Rule of the Door. No further. He carried two of the sheets to have impressions made, sadly returned the originals to the Sacred Archives, and sought out the Prime Minister.

"I have found the content of the Rule of the Door," he announced.

"Excellent! Your name shall appear high on the next achievement citations. What is the content?"

Skarn bowed. "I do not entirely understand it, but this much is apparent: the Rule of the Door consists of—a Door. Here. I have copies of the notes of the Great Kom."

The Prime Minister squinted uncomprehendingly at the ancient script. "It is a fitting tribute to the logic of the Great Kom that the Rule of the Door should consist of a Door. You can read this?"

"Much of it is clear to me," Skarn admitted cautiously.

"I see. And the diagram. Now this would be an ancient model of a matter transmitter."

"Naturally. And this, you see, is the Door. The desired specimen steps through the Door and is immediately transmitted—perhaps to a self-sealing specimen bottle."

"The Door appears to be exceedingly complicated."

"Naturally. It involves, you see, a thought-wave analyzer and a subconsciousness prober. This instrument would appear to be an ancient model of a personality computer. The other components are strange to me, but I assume that this one is a data analyzer which will make the final decision."

"Amazing!"

"In his inestimable wisdom, the Great Kom realized that the disruption of the life process of an intelligent being was not a project to be undertaken impulsively. He formulated a series of maxims: 'Spare the humble one, for his nature is sublime. Spare the wise one, for his nature is rare. Spare the one who loves others more than himself, for love is the ultimate meaning of life. Spare the head of a family, for his loss would injure many. Spare the weak, for their weakness renders them harmless. Spare the generous, for their acts merit generosity.' There is much more. Some of it I do not understand."

"The Rule of the Door must be extremely difficult to apply," the Prime Minister mused.

"Praise be to the Great Kom, we do not have to apply the Rule. We have only to assemble the Door, and the Door will select a proper specimen for his Imperial Majesty."

The Prime Minister thumped his feet gleefully. "Excellent! You will proceed at once to this planet and put the Door in operation."

The citizens of Centertown, Indiana, were agog with excitement. A fabulous mansion was being erected on the outskirts of their fair community by a retired Texas oil millionaire. Or a maharaja who had escaped from his irate subjects with a fortune and a few paltry dozen of his wives and was settling in Indiana. Or a wealthy manufacturer who was going to develop Centertown into a sprawling metropolis.

At any rate, *someone* was building it, price no object, and he was in a hurry. Centertown was sorely taxed to supply the necessary labor force. Men were imported from Terre Haute, and an Indianapolis contractor put in a winding asphalt drive through the trees to the top of the wooded hill where the house was taking shape. On Sunday afternoons the citizens of Centertown turned out en masse to inspect and comment on the week's progress.

When the structure neared completion, the general reaction was one of disillusionment. Its architecture was conservative. Several of Centertown's moderately wealthy boasted more elaborate dwellings. The mysterious mansion proved to be, in disappointing fact, merely another large house.

But the inside—ah, *there* was something to talk about! The good citizens of Centertown hung eagerly on the words of the carpenters who described it. There was no basement, and except for a lavatory and a small utilities room, most of the first floor was a vast living room.

And the owner had a positive mania for closets and doors. Along one entire wall of that spacious living room were closets, large, windowless closets. Their doors were structural monstrosities, fully two feet thick, that functioned strangely and were hung with a strange type of hinge none of the carpenters had ever seen before. And the doors opened inward. Who ever heard of a closet with a door that opened inward? There were eleven of them, and the central closet was left unfinished and doorless.

Clearly, this new resident of Centertown was a most peculiar person. If the workmen were to be believed, he even *looked* peculiar. The painters, returning from putting finishing touches on the living room, added another wrinkle to the mystery. Overnight a door had been placed on the central closet. A locked door.

Skarn Skukarn, Jonathan Skarn to the citizens of Centertown, took up his residence in the new house on a crisp fall day and led a newly arrived, shivering assistant on a tour of inspection. Skarn's pleasure in the house was more than offset by his displeasure with the assistant. The squat, ill-tempered Dork Diffack was grumpy, insulting and generally obnoxious. Skarn confidently expected that he would add treachery to these sterling qualities at the first opportunity; would in fact be immensely pleased if he could bring about Skarn's failure, since the whole disgrace would be Skarn's.

Praise be to the Great Kom, Skarn also knew that he could not fail.

Dork snorted disdainfully as they completed their circuit of the grounds. "Abominable climate," he growled. "And these barbarians—I must admit they have intelligence, since they have a civilization of sorts, but it can't be much intelligence."

"Nevertheless," Skarn said, "they are intelligent, so the Rule of the Door must apply."

"Intolerable nonsense. Why go to all this bother and expense to collect one specimen? Why not just pack one off and have done with it? There are enough of the creatures running around here." Dork glanced toward the highway, where several cars were parked, their occupants staring at the house. "The patrol captain could have done it," he went on. "He should have done it. It's a pretty mess when men of our distinction have to go chasing around the galaxy just to satisfy old Kegor's whims about his Biological Museum."

"His Imperial Majesty does not have whims!" Skarn said sternly.

Dork, being a native of Huzz, one of the Empire's outlying worlds, frequently displayed a boorish, provincial disrespect for His Imperial Majesty. He also displayed disrespect for Skarn, but that was motivated by jealousy over the fact that Skarn's professorship at the Royal University was vastly superior to the one Dork held on Huzz. Dork was competent enough, however, and praise be to the Great Kom, the assignment shouldn't take long.

"I never heard of this Rule of the Door on Huzz," Dork said.

"There had been no reason for its use for so long that it was almost forgotten on the Mother Planet," Skarn said. "It seems to have been invoked only once, and that during the Great Kom's lifetime."

They entered the house and crossed the expanse of living room. Dork gave the Door a peevish kick. "Built precisely to the Great Kom's specifications, I suppose."

"Precisely."

"Well, you said the servants will be here tomorrow. Maybe one of them will blunder through it and then we can go home."

Skarn smiled. "It won't be quite that simple. The qualifications are rather restrictive, you know."

"I have read the content of the Rule," Dork said haughtily. "Do you imagine for one moment that these barbarians possess such qualities as love and wisdom and generosity?"

"Yes," Skarn said. "Yes, I do."

"Anyway, that's not our problem. The Door will decide."

"Perhaps. The Great Kom designed the Door for the inhabitants of a world that is unknown to us. These—ah—barbarians may have an entirely different mental structure. That would mean that we would have to adapt the Door to them, and I must confess that I don't know how to go about it. Some of the instrumentation is exceedingly strange."

"How do you know the Great Kom did not design the Door for the inhabitants of this world?"

"I suppose that is possible," Skarn said doubtfully. "I hadn't thought of it."

"Everything else is arranged?"

"Completely. We have only to throw the activating switch. The relay stations are set up and operating. Once the Door accepts a specimen, it is immediately transmitted all the way to the Royal Museum. It is sealed into a specimen bottle before it knows what's happened, and that's the end of it."

"Then our only problem will be adapting the Door to the specimen."

Skarn took a package of cigarettes, fumbled awkwardly with a cigarette lighter and got one lit. He puffed deeply and went into a paroxysm of coughing. Dork glared disdainfully, but Skarn ignored him. He found the taste abominable and the effect on his throat distressing, but the idea of blowing smoke from his mouth and nose fascinated him. He had seen a carpenter blow smoke rings, and he was determined to acquire that skill himself. He *would* acquire it, even if he had to transport a quantity of these odd objects back to the Royal University and spend the remainder of his life span practicing.

"I don't know that the Door will have to be adapted," he said. "I only acknowledge that possibility. We must expose the Door to a large number of these creatures and study the reactions of the instruments. If the reactions are normal, we should be able to proceed. If not, perhaps suitable adjustments will occur to us."

Dork sneered. "And I suppose these creatures will willingly present themselves to us for study. We have only to issue an invitation and they will come and form a line at the Door."

"Something like that," Skarn agreed. "We merely announce an odd ceremony which these natives call 'open house.' It seems to be a well-established custom. I understand that a great many natives will respond eagerly."

"I suppose there's no harm in trying it," Dork said grudgingly.

The entire population of Centertown and the surrounding countryside turned out for Jonathan Skarn's open house. The wooded hill was packed with cars, the highway was lined with parked cars, and the State Police had to call in reinforcements to keep traffic moving.

Jonathan Skarn, eccentric old gentleman that he was, stationed himself in the front yard, greeted all the visitors warmly, and told them to go right in and make themselves at home. This they did, and after a rapacious assault on the heavily laden refreshment tables, they swarmed through the house.

Though the occasion had to be termed an overwhelming social success, the guests, without exception, emerged disappointed. The door to the upstairs was kept locked. The utilities room and the lavatory were, after all, just a utilities room and a lavatory. And the living room, for all its unusual size and expensive furnishings, was not, as a bright high school student remarked, anything to write home about.

Since the quaint Mr. Skarn remained outside, and since the servants were busily engaged in supplying the refreshment tables—without, however, neglecting to keep the upstairs door locked—the guests pried into all of the strange, empty closets, marveled at the thick doors, and congregated in large numbers around the center door that looked exactly like the others but refused to open.

Upstairs in the laboratory, Dork disgustedly watched their antics in a viewer and kept a sharp eye on his humming instruments; and at the end of the day he announced to Skarn that they had collected sufficient data.

The last of the guests had departed, the servants had restored a semblance of order and wearily headed homeward, and Skarn and Dork relaxed on hassocks in the laboratory and studied the information that drifted slowly across a wall screen.

"These creatures are little more than animals," Dork declared. "But then, that was precisely what I expected. Consider their hideous patches of hair, and their odors, and the fact that they occasionally kill one another, individually or collectively. They hate, they are dominated by greed and jealousy, and I'd say that they're totally lacking in wisdom. Most of all, they lust. They sicken me—every one of them. I didn't find a single worthy creature in the entire pack."

Skarn was attempting to smoke a cigar. His natural bluish tint had deepened to a violent purple, and he felt ill. He coughed out a cloud of smoke and regarded the cigar warily.

"Then our task should be a simple one," he remarked.

"You," Dork exclaimed, "are fully as disgusting as these natives! Must you do that?"

"It is important that we understand the ways of these creatures," Skarn said complacently.

"Surely we can understand them without degrading ourselves!"

Skarn deposited the cigar butt in an ashtray. A touch of a button and it disappeared. The apparent ingenuity of the device, and its basic crudeness, delighted him.

"Whatever else these creatures may be," he said, "they are not simple." He reached for another cigar.

"I tested the Door this morning with the servants," Dork said.

Skarn whirled about incredulously, dropping his cigar. "Without consulting me?"

"It rejected them. I've noticed how they try to open it, now and then, perhaps thinking we may have left it unlocked. So, while they were arranging the food, I activated the Door. Both of them tried it."

"Of course!" Skarn said scornfully. "Why do you think I had this house built? These creatures are intelligent. That means they are curious. There isn't one of them, young or old, who wouldn't attempt to open my mysterious Door if he had a chance. But I want this understood—I am in charge of this assignment. The Door is not to be activated except by my orders."

Dork's eyes gleamed hatred, but he gestured indifferently. "How many glims do we sit around waiting for you to make up your mind?"

"We must proceed cautiously. If the Door had accepted one servant with the other present—"

"What does it matter? We can make our own departure as soon as we've found a specimen. We'll leave nothing that would reveal our origin."

"No," Skarn said. "We must not attract suspicion to ourselves. There must be no witnesses when the Door accepts a specimen. And after that we must wait a suitable period of time so that our departure will not be connected with the disappearance. These creatures may some day learn to transmit themselves. We must not leave an impression that they have enemies on other worlds. Those are stern orders from His Imperial Highness himself."

"So what do you propose to do?"

Skarn unlocked his desk and removed an enormous stack of papers. He plunked it onto the floor, restacked it when it toppled over, and sat back regarding it wearily.

"I located a peculiarly functioning organization called a *detective agency*. It is furnishing me with detailed reports on these creatures. We need only to study each report and ask ourselves, is this subject humble? Is he wise? Is he the head of a family? And so on. We shall select the few who seem best-qualified and invite them, one at a time, to be our guests. Their curiosity will impel them to try the Door. It will certainly accept one of them. After a suitable waiting period to divert suspicion from ourselves, we can dispose of this dwelling and leave."

"It is well arranged," Dork conceded enviously. "But what a frightful bother just to capture a specimen for old Kegor!"

The Door's instruments—those Skarn and Dork were familiar with—reacted normally to the open house guests. Those with which they were not familiar reacted, but normally or not they could not say. They tested the transmitter relay, sending through a stray dog, a cat, and an assortment of live creatures that Skarn obtained from a neighboring farmer.

The Director of the Royal Museum responded promptly. All specimens received in excellent condition and already on display. His Imperial Majesty highly pleased. Now—where was the specimen of the intelligent creature?

Skarn advised the Director to expect it momentarily. He closed the Door and attached a small metal plate that advised, "*Push.*" He activated it and stood nearby, listening to the barely perceptible purring of the instruments. He cautiously tested it on himself and found that it would not open. Everything was ready.

With Dork, he spent hours sifting through the stack of reports. Three-fourths of the citizens were eliminated immediately, a figure that Skarn thought spoke well for these natives. The remaining fourth they studied, compared and debated. They reduced their list to a hundred names, to fifty, and finally to ten. Each of the ten they compared conscientiously with the maxims of the Great Kom. In the end they had four names.

"I don't think this was necessary," Dork said. "But perhaps you are right. This may be the more efficient approach. Certainly the Door will accept any of these."

Skarn nodded and shuffled the reports. He was learning to smoke a pipe, and already the effort had cost him five teeth. New teeth had not yet grown in, and his gums pained him as he grimly mouthed the pipestem. Whenever he used his hand to support the pipe's bowl, he burned himself. He bit down hard on the stem, winced painfully, removed it. His attempted smoke ring poured forth in a turbulent cloud.

He read the four reports again. The Honorable Ernest Schwartz, Mayor of Centertown. Married. He and his wife hated each other devoutly. He had no children, no family dependent upon him. There were multitudinous rumors about him, to be gleaned everywhere in Centertown and environs. He was a liar. He was also a thief. He had betrayed the trust of his office repeatedly to enrich himself. He had betrayed his friends. He was greedy and evil and held affection for no one. He had carried on what the natives boorishly called *love affairs* with the wives of his friends, and pushed his own wife into an affair for his political advantage. He seemed to bewitch the voters at election time.

Skarn frowned. *Election* time? He would have to investigate that. Whatever it meant, bewitching the voters seemed an immoral thing to do.

He turned to the next report. Sam White, Centertown Chief of Police. A bachelor with no known relatives. He kept his job, it was said, by cooperating with the mayor's crooked schemes. Some of his police officers called him a petty tyrant. He was adept at obtaining confessions. He had several times been accused of brutality toward prisoners.

Jim Adams, the Centertown drunk. He never worked, lived off his wife's meager earnings, and beat his wife and family mercilessly, drunk or sober. Technically he was the head of a family; in actuality his family would be far better off without him.

Elmer Harley, a ne'er-do-well mechanic. A good mechanic, it was said, when he worked at it. He had been convicted and served jail terms for several crimes. Terre Haute police had given him a standing order to stay out of town. Centertown tolerated him warily. He had no family and no friends. He worked when he could, if he felt like it, at either of Centertown's two garages. One of the proprietors liked him, it was said, because he was adroit at padding repair bills. That proprietor would have stood high on Skarn's list had it not been for the fact that he verifiedly loved his wife and children.

"When do we start?" Dork asked.

Skarn removed his pipe from his lips and made another blundering attempt at a smoke ring. "Tomorrow. I'll ask this Mayor Schwartz to have dinner with me."

The Honorable Ernest Schwartz entered Skarn's enormous living room with the air of belonging there. A big man, hearty, robust, his hair shining black despite his sixty years, his booming voice and laugh seemed to conjure up unnatural echoes, as though some left over from the open house had been lying inert behind the furniture awaiting a clarion invocation. The mayor had the voice for it. While Skarn was placing his coat, hat and cane in one of the closets, his commonplace compliments about the house filled the living room and shook every somnolent echo into wakefulness.

Skarn turned, absently rubbing his ears, and regarded the mayor strangely. He was seeing him, not as the Honorable Mayor of Centertown, Indiana, but as a specimen in sealed plastic in the Royal Museum. He was seeing him as one of a long row of bottled monstrosities that His Imperial Majesty's patrol ships had sent in from a multitude of planets. He was seeing His Imperial Majesty himself, cackling with delight, leading a noisy crowd of visiting dignitaries through the displays and stopping to point out Mayor Schwartz's ridiculous black hair, his smug little mustache, his flamboyant clothing, the sparkling cuff links, the gold chain that hung from his vest pockets.

It seemed wrong. Alien though he was, Skarn could sense the man's personal charm. He was friendly. He was obviously intelligent.

Skarn shrugged. The decision was not his to make. The Door would decide.

"Excuse me, please," he said. "I do not like to entertain with servants around. I'll bring the food myself. If you'll make yourself comfortable—"

"Why, certainly," Schwartz boomed. "Anything I can do to help?"

"No, thank you. I can manage nicely."

Skarn joined Dork in the laboratory, and the two of them sat watching Schwartz in the viewer. Dork was jubilant.

"What a specimen he'll make!" he exulted. "He's a big one. Do you suppose the specimen bottle will hold him?"

"It held that thing they call a calf," Skarn said.

Schwartz had taken a seat, but the reflected light from the sign on the Door caught his attention. He calmly got to his feet, crossed the room and read the label. The sign instructed him to push. He pushed. The Door resisted firmly.

Dork explosively released a series of involved Huzzian oaths. "Why? Why? There isn't a creature in our files better qualified than this one!"

Skarn said thoughtfully, "So it would seem. We must have made a mistake. Perhaps I can find out what it was. If you'd care to take notes—"

"Not me. He *shouts*. Even with the volume turned down he gives me a headache. I'm going to bed."

Skarn wheeled a serving cart into the living room. The mayor hurriedly got to his feet and helped him place the dishes on the table. They took their places, and Skarn poured the cocktails.

The mayor raised his glass and said seriously, "May your residence in Centertown be a long and happy one."

"Thank you," Skarn said, feeling strangely moved.

The mayor sniffed hungrily as Skarn uncovered the dishes. He said with a sly grin, "I have a confession to make. The reason I jumped at this invitation was because I knew you'd hired Lucy Morgan."

Skarn said indifferently, "She seems capable." He found the native foods so strange that he had to measure the cooks' skills in terms of more or less indigestion.

"Man, she's marvelous!" the mayor exclaimed. "She used to work for me."

"Indeed? But if you like the food she prepares, why didn't you keep her in your employment?"

The mayor scowled. "Women get funny notions. That was years ago. Lucy was in her early twenties, and my wife couldn't get it through her head that it was Lucy's cooking that I was interested in. Are you married?"

"Not now," Skarn answered cautiously.

The mayor nodded and helped himself to steak. He concentrated on his food and talked little between mouthfuls, mainly about Centertown. Skarn ate sparsely and tried to appear interested.

"I appreciate this," the mayor said suddenly. "Don't often get a quiet evening. The mayor's time belongs to everyone, day or night. Complaints about taxes, or the garbage service, or a hole in the street, or anything else. Each time I'm elected I swear it'll be the last time. But here I am—ten straight terms and I'll probably go on until I die. Unless the voters decide to throw me out."

"*To throw you—*" Skarn paused. "I see. You were expressing it symbolically. I don't understand these elections of yours. We don't have them where I come from."

"I figured you were one of those refugees. Well, it seems simple to us, but I suppose it really isn't. Two or three men run for mayor, and the people vote their choice, and the one that gets the most votes is elected. For two years. Then there's another election and the defeated candidates try again. Or maybe some new candidates. All it amounts to is that the people decide who runs things—those of them that take the trouble to vote."

"This voting is not required?"

"Purely voluntary. Sometimes the turnout isn't so hot."

Skarn considered this with a deep frown. "Wouldn't it be simpler just to have your—" He thought for a moment and attempted a translation. "Have your Director of Vocational Assignments appoint a mayor?"

"You're thinking of the city manager sort of thing," the mayor said. "Some places have them, but it's usually the city council that does the appointing. Those places usually have mayors, too."

Skarn squirmed uncomfortably and tried again. "Your Director of Vocational Assignments—"

"We haven't got anything like that."

"Then who assigns the vocations?"

"Nobody. People work at what they want, if they can get it, and if they can't they work at what they can get. It isn't like those Iron Curtain countries. If a man doesn't like his job, or his boss, or if he can get something better, he quits. The people run the show here. Sometimes they get the wool pulled over their eyes, but not for long."

"And—you're going to be mayor until you die?"

"I suppose it'll work out that way, unless the people throw me out."

"When are you going to die?"

The mayor winced. "For God's sake!" He dissolved in laughter, booming out great, reverberating rolls of sound until he gasped for breath. "How do I know? I might get hit by a car on the way home, or drop dead from overeating. Or I might live to be a hundred. What a question!"

Skarn leaned back to stare at the mayor. Ideas were coming at him so fast that he could not get a grip on them, and his thoughts whirled dizzily.

"I came up the hard way," the mayor said. "I made my money honestly and I went into politics honestly. I've kept my hands about as clean as a politician can. Most of the people know that, which is why they vote for me. It's petty politics. I'm just a big frog in a small puddle, but I like it that way. I know everyone personally and everyone knows me. Every time a new baby is born, I have a new boss. I'm as happy as the proud parents. I wouldn't have it any other way.

"But politics is a dirty business. Some people had it all their own way in this town before I was elected, and they'd like to have it that way again. They've pulled every foul trick in the books, and some so low that no book would be nasty enough to mention them. They spread the damnedest lies about me, and my wife just can't take that. We were happily married until I got elected mayor, but now—I suppose anything a man accomplishes has its price, but if I had it to do over again, I don't know." Suddenly he grinned. "I'll tell you what—I've got a book on the American system of government. I'll send it over. It explains things a lot better than I could tell them to you."

"I would appreciate that," Skarn said. "I would appreciate that very much."

Chief of Police Sam White arrived on foot to be Skarn's luncheon guest. A tall, slim, dignified man, his manner was soft-spoken, his eyes hard and searching but none the less friendly. Skarn, on the basis of his report, had visualized him in some dismal dungeon furiously lashing a prisoner, and the chief did not seem to belong in that role. Silvery-gray hair crowned a wrinkled, sympathetic face. There was gentleness in his handshake, in his mannerisms, in his voice. Skarn began to visualize him in a different setting—in a sealed specimen bottle—and felt uncomfortable.

Skarn left him alone in the living room, and he and Dork

watched anxiously from the laboratory. The chief shocked them thoroughly—he seated himself and waited quietly without so much as a glance in the direction of the mysterious Door. Later Skarn lured him into making the attempt by asking his assistance in opening it. And the Door ignored him.

After lunch they sat together on the sofa and talked and smoked, the chief describing his various hobbies with dry humor and Skarn listening intently. Did Skarn ever do any fishing? Or hunting?

"I'll take you with me the next time I go out," the chief said. "If you're interested, that is." Skarn was interested. "Ever play any chess?" Skarn did not know the game. "Drop in sometime when you're uptown. Things are usually pretty quiet around the police department of a town this size. I'll teach you."

The chief sent a smoke ring sailing across the room, and Skarn looked after it enviously. His own effort was a formless catastrophe.

When Skarn had stopped coughing, the chief said gently, "You go at it the wrong way. You can't form a smoke ring by blowing. You have to do it with your mouth. Look."

Skarn watched, made the effort, failed miserably.

"Try it again," the chief suggested.

Skarn tried. His tenth attempt was a definite smoke ring, wobbly, lopsided and short-lived, but still a ring. Skarn watched it with delight.

"Keep working at it," the chief said. "A little practice and you'll be an expert."

"I will," Skarn promised fervently, and felt forever beholden to him.

Afterward, Dork stormed angrily about the laboratory while Skarn restudied his reports. "The detective agency is in error," Skarn announced. "Those men are not evil."

"They're evil," Dork said, "but they're important. They have positions of responsibility. The Door may consider that."

"True."

"The other two have no importance whatsoever."

"True."

"So let's get on with it. We only need one specimen."

Jim Adams arrived early that evening. He was wearing his best—or only—dress suit, a shabby, threadbare garment that flapped loosely on his slight form, but he'd forgotten to shave. He extended a trembling hand for Skarn to shake, and then, fixing the eyes of the utterly damned on him, whined, "I need a drink. Haven't had one today. Will you give me a drink?"

Skarn patted his shoulder gently. "Of course. You can have all you want." He led the slight, stumbling figure across the living room. "I keep it there—in the center closet. You help yourself while I'm getting the food."

Adams pushed at the door, beat on it, hurled his scant weight against it, shrieked and kicked and clawed and finally slumped to the floor sobbing brokenly. Skarn and Dork's disgust abruptly changed to disbelief. The Door was rejecting him.

Skarn returned with the food and a supply of liquor, and Adams ate little and drank much, drank himself into a reeking, slobbering intoxication and collapsed. Skarn examined his unconscious body doubtfully and finally became sufficiently alarmed to call Sam White.

"I have Jim Adams here for dinner," he said, "and—"

The chief chuckled. "Say no more. I'll send someone to collect him."

A police officer hauled away Adams's inert form, leaving Skarn both relieved and puzzled.

"And just how do you account for the Door not taking *him?*" Dork demanded.

"I don't," Skarn said. "I can't account for it at all."

Elmer Harley arrived in a belligerent mood, thumping rudely on the door, making no motion to accept Skarn's outstretched hand, and ignoring his invitation to enter. "Mind telling me why you asked me out here?"

"I'm getting acquainted with some of the people of Centertown," Skarn said uneasily. "I hope that the invitation does not offend you."

Harley shrugged and offered his hand. "Just wondered. I heard you had Jim Adams here, and let him drink himself to the gills."

"Yes, but—"

"And before that you entertained the mayor and Sam White?"

"Yes."

"And now me. It doesn't make sense."

"How much of life does make sense?"

Harley grinned. "You said a mouthful there," he announced bitterly.

He followed Skarn into the living room. "I'll bring in the food," Skarn said. "The liquor is in the middle closet. Pick out what you'd like to have."

A moment later, watching from the laboratory, Skarn and Dork saw him push once on the Door, hard, and then walk over to a sofa and sit down.

Dork stomped off to his bedroom, and Skarn returned to the living room with the serving cart.

"The door's locked," Harley said.

"It doesn't have a lock," Skarn replied. "I'm afraid it's stuck. I've been having trouble with it."

Harley bounced to his feet. "That so? I'll take a look at it."

He applied his shoulder to the Door. A moment later he backed away, red-faced and breathing heavily. "It's really stuck. If you have some tools, I'll see what I can do about it."

"It's not that important," Skarn said.

Harley stepped to the next closet. He pushed the thick door inward and peered admiringly at the hinges. "That's really slick. Slides the door back and then lets it open. Never saw anything like it. Is the other door hung like this one?"

"Why, yes," Skarn said.

Harley moved the door slowly, watching the action of the hinges. "That's really slick," he said again. "I don't see how anything could have gone wrong. Did you make these things yourself?"

Skarn maintained an embarrassed silence.

"You ought to patent them. There might be some money in it."

"Our food will be getting cold," Skarn said.

"No kidding. Safes and refrigerators, things with thick doors —they could use a hinge like that. If I was you, I'd patent it."

"Thank you for the suggestion. I'll consider it."

Harley ate hungrily, accepting second and third helpings, and afterward he relaxed and talked about automobiles. Skarn listened attentively and managed an occasional smoke ring.

Harley knew automobiles. He discussed them collectively and individually, their good points and weak points, their trade-in values, their economy or lack of it, where they were most likely to break down and why.

"When you get around to buying a car," he said, "ask me. I can keep you from going wrong on a new one, and if it's a used one, I can tell you if you're getting your money's worth."

"I'll remember that," Skarn promised. "I've heard that you are a very good mechanic."

"I get by."

"With so many automobiles to work on, a good mechanic should do well."

"Not in Centertown," Harley said grimly. "Not unless he's willing to go along with the crooks that own the garages."

Skarn studied him bewilderedly. He was a muscular man of medium height. His suit was worn but freshly pressed, his dark hair neatly trimmed. The fine scar line that curved around his left cheek was noticeable but not disfiguring. He was clean-shaven. He looked *respectable*.

Skarn could not envision him as the man the report described.

Nor in a specimen bottle. "If you had your life to live over," he said, "is there anything you'd do differently?"

Harley smiled wistfully. "There isn't much that I wouldn't do differently."

"For example?"

"I pulled a couple of jobs when I was young. Small stuff, but I did some time. Now, whenever anything happens, the police come looking for me. Ex-con, you know. I can't get a decent job. I shouldn't have come back to Centertown, but my mother was here, and just coming out of the pen that way I couldn't make a home for her anywhere else. She died four years ago and I'm still here. In a rut."

Dork had returned to the laboratory. Skarn found him there after Harley left, glumly looking at the view of the darkened living room. "I heard," Dork said. "He loved his mother. That is considered an overpowering virtue among these creatures."

"Perhaps so," Skarn said.

"Invite one of them back," Dork urged earnestly. "Any one. We can put the Door on manual and shove him through and have done with it. This planet will be a better place, and in Old Kegor's museum he'll at least have some slight ornamental value. And we can go home."

"No!" Skarn said sharply. "We must not contest the wisdom of the Great Kom."

"Then what *are* you going to do?"

"I don't know. I must think the matter out carefully. Perhaps there are no evil creatures in Centertown, and we must search elsewhere."

Dork got to his feet and paced back and forth, his squat figure leaning forward at a tense angle, his eyes blazing angrily, his face a violent shade of blue. "All right," he said finally. "You are in charge. But I am going to invite more of these creatures here to try the Door. You can't deny me that."

"No," Skarn agreed. "I see no objection to that, as long as you invite them one at a time. You may use the reports and invite anyone you like."

In the morning there was a confidential message for Skarn. Dork Diffark had sent in an alarming complaint on Skarn's management of his assignment, alleging that Skarn was de-liberately delaying the selection of a proper specimen and displaying a suspicious penchant for native customs. The Prime Minister demanded an explanation.

Skarn replied with a report on Dork's treasonable suggestion that a specimen be obtained without the Door's approval. He installed a mental lock on the master control, so Dork could not place the Door on manual operation without Skarn's consent. For the moment Skarn's position was secure, but he had a queasy feeling that time might be running out on him. His Imperial Majesty was not noted for his patience.

Skarn walked to Centertown and wandered in and out of the stores, making casual purchases and attempting to engage the clerks in conversation. It puzzled him that they were, every one of them, obsessed with the weather. He could understand that a relatively primitive civilization that had not mastered weather control might regard the atmospheric conditions with awe and frustration, but he could not understand why every individual seemed to take a personal responsibility for it being the kind of day it was.

"Nice day," they would say. Or, "It sure is nice out." Or, "Lovely day, isn't it?"

When Skarn attempted to direct the conversation into other channels, he was politely but firmly rebuffed. He would make his purchase and ask, "Do you know Jim Adams?"

"Who doesn't?" the clerk would say and move on to the next customer.

"Do I know Chief White?" a shoeshine boy said. "I ain't no criminal!"

"What do I think of the mayor?" a waitress said. "I aim to vote for him. Another cup of coffee?"

"Why—ah—yes," Skarn said, and drank it, though it nauseated him.

The natives he had invited to his home had talked volubly with him. Those he encountered about town were friendly enough if Skarn approached them first, but their restraint baffled him. What could account for such a fundamental difference in their behavior? It was a matter for profound psychological speculation.

Skarn ate a revolting lunch at the drugstore and then cautiously descended the worn steps to the basement of the rickety city hall where police headquarters was located. Sam White was alone in the small headquarters room, chair tilted back, his feet resting comfortably on his desk.

He nodded casually and pointed at a chair. "What brings you to the law?"

"I am making a social call," Skarn said politely.

"Make yourself comfortable. Not many people come down here unless they have something to beef about."

"I suppose you meet more than your share of evil people," Skarn said.

"I wouldn't say that. I really don't believe there is such a thing as an evil person. We get some bad ones now and then, but there isn't a one of them who couldn't have been straightened out if someone had taken him in hand before he got too far out of line."

"Do you really believe that?"

The chief smiled. "'There is so much good in the worst of us, and so much bad in the best of us, that it hardly behooves any of us to talk about the rest of us.' I might have written that myself if someone hadn't beaten me to it."

"Do you *really* believe that?" Skarn persisted.

"Of course I do. Sometimes it's the only thing that keeps me going."

"And yet you sometimes find it necessary to use violence on your prisoners."

Chief White's feet hit the floor with a crash. "Nobody in this department uses violence on anybody!"

"But I heard—"

"Sure, you heard. You hear that about police anywhere. That's a crook's last line of defense. Catch him good and the only out he can think of is to try to blame something on the police. We have to be pretty damned careful to keep them from getting away with it."

"I see," Skarn said meekly.

The chief returned his feet to his desk, and Skarn lit a cigarette and sent a perfect smoke ring floating across the room. The chief whistled.

"You've got that down pat. What did I tell you?"

"Your prediction was profoundly accurate."

"I'll make another prediction. I think you'll like chess. Want to learn?"

Skarn watched curiously while the chief got out the board and arranged the oddly shaped pieces. "This," the chief said, holding up a black one, "is a knight."

Skarn reached for a white one with identical shape. "And I suppose this is a day."

The chief flapped his arms and howled, and Skarn laughed with him, wondering why.

It was dusk when Skarn walked slowly back up the hill. Dork was entertaining a guest—a female guest. Skarn slipped up the stairway unnoticed and activated the living room viewer. He had carefully avoided the native females in his own tests. Their psychology seemed infinitely more complex than that of the males, and their motives shrouded in fantastic obscurity.

After a brief discussion Dork gave money to his female specimen, and she walked resolutely to the Door and shoved against it. It failed to open. A violent argument followed, and she flung the money at Dork and left.

Dork did not offer to discuss the incident, and Skarn did not ask him about it.

The stores were not yet open when Skarn reached Centertown the next morning. He walked the length of Main Street and back again, surprised at the number of familiar faces that he met. Jim Adams was slouched in front of the Center Bar, and when Skarn passed him a second time he squinted uncertainly and wiped a trembling hand across his eyes. "Oh, it's you," he said.

"Nice morning, isn't it?" Skarn found that he slipped into

the native pattern of conversation with disconcerting ease. "This place will open in a few minutes. May I buy you a drink?"

Adams said nothing. They were the first customers, and Skarn followed Adams to the bar, paid for the drink he ordered, and watched as he downed it greedily.

"Another?" Skarn suggested.

Adams wiped his mouth with the back of his hand and stared blankly at him. Skarn nodded at the bartender, who re-filled the glass. Slumped over the bar, Adams gazed at it dumbly. Suddenly he clutched it and flung the contents into Skarn's face.

"I'm killing myself fast enough," he said bitterly. "I don't need your help."

Skarn accepted a paper napkin from the bartender and dried his face. "Let's sit down," he said. "Is there something you'd rather have? Food, maybe?"

He led Adams over to a booth.

Adams said incredulously, "You ain't sore?"

"I think," Skarn said, "that you are a very sick man."

Adams buried his face in his arms and sobbed. "When I ain't drunk, I'm a louse because I want to get drunk. And when I'm drunk I'm a louse."

"Isn't there anything you can do about it?"

"In this hick town? Big cities got Alcoholics Anonymous and things like that. Here there ain't nothing. Doc Winslow says go in the hospital and get cured, but that costs money an' I ain't got money. Won't ever have none unless I get cured, an' I can't get cured unless I have some. So I drink myself to death. Who the hell cares?"

Skarn got to his feet and took a firm grip on Adams's arm. "Let's go and talk with your Doctor Winslow," he said.

Doctor Winslow made a series of long-distance telephone calls and struggled valiantly to describe hospital expenses in terms understandable to Skarn. Then he jovially slapped Adams on the back and shook Skarn's hand. And at noon Skarn was at the railroad station seeing that a somewhat bewildered Adams got aboard the train that would take him to a hospital.

Mrs. Adams was there, a slight, pale-faced woman, and with her were the seven Adams children. Mrs. Adams sank to her knees before Skarn and clutched his legs tearfully. Skarn gently raised her to her feet.

"It's all right," Skarn said. "Jim is going to come back cured. Aren't you, Jim?"

"I sure am," Adams promised.

"He's been a sick man, but he's going to be all right. And then your worries will be over."

"God bless you," Mrs. Adams sobbed.

Skarn patted her shoulder awkwardly. "If you need anything in the meantime," he heard himself say, "don't hesitate to call on me."

As soon as the train left Skarn walked over to the Centertown Bank and arranged to have a weekly allowance paid to the Adams family. Coming out of the bank he met Chief of Police White.

White's hand clamped painfully on Skarn's. "I heard about what you did," he said.

They walked together along Main Street. The president of the bank stopped to shake hands with Skarn. Faces familiar and unfamiliar smiled and spoke pleasantly. In one block Skarn was offered seven free beers, three dinners and a lodge membership.

"What's happened?" he asked bewilderedly.

White grinned at him. "In a town this size, word gets around fast. Jim Adams has been kind of a civic problem for years. Everyone felt responsible for him, but nobody knew what to do about him. You solved the problem at one crack. That's what's happened."

They paused in front of the city hall, and White gripped Skarn's hand again. "These small towns are peculiar places," he said. "A person can come from the outside and live in one for years and never make the grade. And then sometimes— well, whether you like it or not, you're one of us."

Mayor Schwartz lumbered up, breathing heavily. "I chased you a block," he panted. "Didn't you hear me calling you?"

"No, I didn't," Skarn said. "I'm very sorry if—"

"Heard what you did for Jim Adams. Wonder why we didn't think of it years ago. Look. We've got a vacancy on the planning commission and I think you're just the man for it. I've talked with the council members, and if it's all right with you we'll make it official at the meeting tonight."

"I'm afraid I don't understand," Skarn confessed.

"It's nothing complicated. The commission meets once a month and mostly just talks. But you're a newcomer and you might see things the rest of us have been overlooking for years, like Jim Adams. Why not give it a try? You can always resign if it's too much of an imposition."

Skarn looked at Chief White. White nodded gravely.

"Why, yes," Skarn said. "I'd be honored."

He found Elmer Harley at work in Merrel's Garage. Harley slammed down a wrench and went over to wash up before he would accept Skarn's hand.

"Naw, nobody will care if I have a beer with you," he said, when Skarn timidly extended the invitation.

They crossed the street to the Center Bar. The bartender brought the beers to their booth, and Skarn took a sip and grimaced.

"I heard what you did for Jim Adams," Harley said. "And—hell, it was a fine thing to do."

"Do you think he'll reform?" Skarn asked.

"With half a chance, I'm sure he will."

"Then it was time someone did something about it."

Harley nodded and took another gulp of beer. "Jim wasn't a bad guy," he said. "He was weak and he got himself trapped. You thinking of reforming me?"

"I *had* given it some thought," Skarn conceded.

"I suppose it's time somebody did something about that, too," Harley said.

"I was thinking of opening a garage. An honest garage. Do you think there's a place for one here?"

"There's a place for an honest garage anywhere."

"Do you think you could run one for me?"

"Try me!"

"See if you can find a place for it, and let me know what you'd need."

"Right away," Harley said. "Just as soon as I tell Merrel to go to hell."

The house was dark when Skarn returned, dark upstairs and down. He moved easily through the darkness to the laboratory, heard Dork's quick breathing, and settled himself on a hassock near him. Dork preferred the darkness. He did not like the confusing alternation of night and day. On his native planet it was always dark or never dark, and Dork claimed that the revolutions of this primitive planet endangered his health.

Skarn lit a cigarette, and Dork winced in the flash of light. "Do you have a specimen ready?" he demanded.

"No," Skarn said. "Do you have one?"

"I heard about what you've been doing. I made a full report, and I have a reply. You are relieved of your assignment and ordered to report to the Mother Planet immediately."

Skarn smiled. "And you are to complete the assignment, I suppose."

"On personal orders from His Imperial Majesty."

"Following the Rule of the Door explicitly, I suppose."

Dork's laughter was hideous. "The Great Kom is beyond caring. As for His Imperial Majesty, when he wants a specimen he *wants* it. He doesn't expect the Rules to be followed; he only wants to be told that they were followed. Your stupidity in the handling of this assignment has been a disgrace, Skarn Skukarn. I very much doubt that you will be permitted to fulfill your span of living."

"Would you mind telling me how you plan to obtain a specimen?"

"I'll invite the specimens you've already selected. Three of them, since you've sent the other away."

"The Door won't accept them. I doubt that it will accept any resident of Centertown."

"The Door will accept them. I'll operate it on manual and

send all three of them through and get away from this cursed planet."

"I have the master control on mental lock. I won't release it to you."

"You'll release it," Dork said grimly. "There are worse penalties than death, you know."

"Yes," Skarn murmured. "Life."

There'd been a lovely young wife whom he loved, and an exalted minister who took her from him, and after that—emptiness. Glim after glim replete with a nonsensical sifting of trivialities. Having nothing else to live for, he'd lived for his work and risen to the top of his profession because he could perform his sifting tirelessly, with no distractions except his memories. It had always been life that he feared—not death. He tried to imagine how it must be for these natives, who left their life spans to chance instead of making them a matter of law.

Condemned to a life without purpose, he had at least maintained his integrity. "These natives are friends of mine," he said. "Skarn Skukarn does not betray a friend."

"I will ask for new equipment," Dork said.

"When I make known the reason for your request, it will be refused."

Dork laughed harshly. "How will you make it known? His Imperial Majesty has not ordered your recall to ask your advice."

Suddenly he leaped to his feet. "What was that?" His hands closed on Skarn's arm. "Did you hear it? Someone is downstairs."

Skarn activated the viewer and flooded the living room with invisible light.

"We have a visitor," Dork hissed. "Skarn—we're being robbed!"

A shabby figure fumbled awkwardly through the darkness, clumsily feeling its way around the furniture. A handkerchief covered the face below the eyes.

"He's heard about our Door," Skarn said. "He probably thinks we keep riches behind it."

Dork cackled gleefully. "Our task is finished. The Door will certainly accept a specimen that approaches it to commit an evil act."

"His evil act may have a noble purpose," Skarn said.

The intruder blundered across the room, lunged into one of the closets, emerged a moment later and felt his way along the wall toward the Door. Dork sucked his breath noisily and released it in a spasm of profanity when the Door failed to move.

"Set the Door on manual," he snarled. "I'll push him through. No one knows he's here. No one will miss him. We can get off this damnable world immediately."

"The Rule of the Door—"

"Damn the Rule! Do you know this native? Do you claim him for a friend?"

"No," Skarn admitted. "I don't know him."

"Set the Door on manual," Dork ordered. The sneering authority in his voice made Skarn cringe. Dork swaggered away, and Skarn sank back wearily.

Truly, the Great Kom had acted with awesome foresight in devising such a Door. Perhaps it was never meant to open. Who could say, after all, that the Imperial Majesty of that ancient time had actually obtained an intelligent specimen? Perhaps in his immortal wisdom the Great Kom had deliberately devised a plan to prevent that. And now this—this *circumventing* of the Door. It was a terrible thing.

Let Dork do his worst, but Skarn would not release the Door to him. He could not.

In the room below, the intruder was assaulting the Door with his shoulder. The lights came on; Dork entered the room, hands raised in mock fear of the thief's clumsy weapon.

"Certainly I'll open it for you," he said. "Come and help me push."

Dork moved toward the door, paused, half-turned to say something.

Suddenly the Door swished open. Dork was sucked through

in an instant, and as the startled thief leaped after him the Door slammed in his face. He beat upon it angrily.

Skarn jerked to his feet, fists clenched, his mind paralyzed with shock. He tried to envision what was happening, knowing that while he thought about it, it had already happened—the body of Dork Diffack whipped at many times the speed of light from relay station to relay station across space and sealed into a specimen bottle at the Royal Museum, to the colossal consternation of the attendants. They would recognize him immediately, of course, but it would be too late.

Skarn bowed humbly to the memory of the Great Kom. Perhaps the Door had been attuned to the characteristics of one people only, the inhabitants of Dork's planet Huzz, discovered back in those remote times when the ships of the Empire were first creeping outward from the Mother Planet. Or perhaps not. But manifestly, the Door had been designed so that only a creature like Dork would be accepted, a creature devoid of love and friendship and kindness, an evil creature surprised in a sinister plot against another intelligent being. The wisdom of the Great Kom was absolute.

Skarn acted quickly. He dared not return to the Mother Planet; but he liked these natives. He admired the freedom they enjoyed and the curious blend of good and bad in their characters. He had many years to live as the natives measured time. He had the allowance of precious metals furnished to him for his assignment. He had the house. He had—yes, in Centertown he had friends.

He opened a panel in the wall and closed the switch that sent the transmitter hurtling back through space. In succession the relay stations would fold in on each other and all return to the Mother Planet. The enraged Imperial Majesty might send an expedition after Skarn, but it didn't matter. Only Dork knew where Skarn had located on this planet, and Dork's knowledge was safe for an eternity. So was Skarn.

He went to the telephone and called Sam White. "I have been reflecting upon that game which you call chess. I believe the next time I can defeat you. Is it too late to try tonight?"

"Hell, no!" White said. "Come on over."

"Shortly," Skarn said. "I have a small matter to attend to here."

The removal of the mechanism had released the door, and the thief was bewilderedly staring into the central closet. Skarn paralyzed him with a nerve gun, took the threatening revolver and released him. The young eyes that stared at him over the handkerchief were terrified.

"What happened to that guy? That closet—it's empty!"

"Of course it's empty," Skarn said. "That's why the door opened so easily. Now tell me, my friend. Why is it that you need money?"

2

PETTY LARCENY

Dear Edna—

I'm writing this to tell you things look pretty good and I'll be back soon and you can start buying that trousseau you been holding out for. Good news—huh, baby? We'll have to get married on the Q.T. and take a long honeymoon for reasons I'll explain. Blackie and I will be holing up for a while so I can't give you a date and I don't want the whole town turning out when I show up. Kind of get things ready but strictly Q.T. Got that?

We finally made our haul and it's so big we been pinching ourselves about it ever since but it's had some funny results. We might have to lay low in Mexico for a few months after we're married but I don't think you'll mind when you hear what happened.

We were moving across Wisconsin pulling that old gag where Blackie trips over something in a store and breaks his arm. A lot of these small storekeepers don't carry insurance and they jump at a fast settlement. We were doing pretty well so when we came to a little resort town we decided to take a short vacation and then hit the local storekeeper on our way out.

Across the road from our motel was a big outdoor cafe right on the lake. It was a hot night and when we walked over to have a nightcap there wasn't a vacant table in the place. A lot of people were standing around waiting so when Blackie spotted two empty chairs we made a run for them. As we were sitting down I asked, "Are these chairs taken?" And this fellow that had a table all to himself said, "Sssertainly not. Pleassse join me."

Knock me down with a corn plaster if it wasn't an alien—trilling voice and hissing s's and all. I'd seen plenty of them from a distance but I'd never had a chance to talk with one. Blackie and I sat back and looked him over and he didn't mind in the least because he was staring just as hard at us.

It wouldn't be so bad if only they didn't think they had to look *human.* Even a classy tailored suit tends to look sloppy when you order it five sizes too large and conceal an extra pair of arms under it. The wigs help some if you look at them from behind but from the front they're just hopeless. I've heard that some of them wear false noses. This one didn't. There was just the row of eyes across where the forehead should have been and the beak down where there should have been a chin and everything in between a big fat scaly nothing.

I told myself we were just as odd to him and after a few drinks he commenced looking almost normal. So that's how Blackie and I came to be making small talk with an alien.

Afterwhile the moon came out and made a right pretty reflection in the lake but I won't pretend I was thinking of you. Not with that alien sitting beside me. I don't think you would have liked that anyway.

It was only a half moon anyway. The alien looked up at it and said, "It isss an odd ssshape."

"I suppose you have five moons going around your world," Blackie said.

"No," the alien said. "We have none. The phenomena isss entirely new to me." He sat looking at it kind of vacantly. "Hasss it alwaysss had that odd ssshape?"

Blackie winked at me. "Of course not. Just since we started

selling it. What you see is the part that hasn't been sold." You
know Blackie. He can work out a business deal in his sleep.
"Care to make a small investment?" he asked.

"In the moon? Isss it expensssive?"

"Not very. How big a slice would you like to buy?"

The alien sat there dead serious looking at the moon. I
managed to keep my face straight.

"I will have to dissscussss this with my brother," he said.
We found out later that all the aliens call each other brother.

"Do that," Blackie said. "Where can I get in touch with
you?"

"In touch? You refer to—we ressside at the Balmy Beach
Resssort."

"I'll give you a call in the morning from our Madison office,"
Blackie said. "Who do I ask for?"

"The name is Sssim."

We introduced ourselves—not our right names—and the alien
bowed like an opera tenor and walked away if the way they
scoot around can be called walking.

"Sim for simple," Blackie said.

"You can't think you're actually going to sell him real estate
on the moon," I said. "He isn't that simple."

Blackie grinned. "I read an article about the aliens by some
doctor or psychoanalyst or some such thing. He says they're a
race of morons that discovered space travel by accident.
Claims they're so stupid that no one can figure out how they
manage to fly those ships."

"But you'll notice they do fly them," I said. "Why would
they buy moon real estate from us? They can get up there and
take as much as they want and we can't get near it."

"Sim for simple," Blackie said. "All it costs us is a trip to
Madison and a phone call. Did you notice he was too stupid
to know anything about the phases of the moon?"

When he put it that way I couldn't very well kick. Nothing
ventured nothing gained and all that sort of thing. We drove
down to Madison in the morning and bought ourselves an op-

tion on the rent of an office with a five buck deposit. Then Blackie called the alien.

He came out of the phone booth grinning. "He's interested," he said. "He'll be at our office at ten tomorrow morning. Now we got work to do."

We put in a frantic day. A sign painter had to be hired to paint SURPLUS PROPERTY DISPOSAL UNIT NO. 437 on the door of our office. I rented office furniture and found a woman willing to pretend to be a secretary for three days if we paid her a week's salary in advance. Blackie went looking for a printer who'd work fast and keep his mouth shut for a price. He came back late that night with a bunch of phony deeds and purchase agreements and receipts and such. He has a flair for that sort of thing.

I spent most of the day trying to find some maps of the moon which in case you've never tried is not an item you can pick up at the corner filling station. I finally got the library to make me some copies of pictures.

The aliens arrived right on schedule the next morning. We hadn't mentioned aliens to the secretary and her face was working in seven different directions when she showed them into the inner office. She by the way was a tough old dame about fifty so you got no cause to be jealous.

The aliens had a couple of things bothering them. During the night they'd taken a run up to the moon to look the property over. They were kind of upset to find the whole moon there. Sim had thought that people were buying chunks and toting them away on account of the odd shape he'd seen from Earth. Blackie talked around that by explaining that we were just lighting up the part that hadn't been sold yet.

As it turned out the real problem was that they didn't want to buy just part of the moon. They wanted the whole thing.

"That *might* be possible," Blackie said thoughtfully. "Of course you'd have to buy back the parts that have already been sold. But if that's what you want—"

That was what they wanted.

"It'll be expensive," Blackie said.

Sim said hang the expenssse.

"It'll be difficult," Blackie said. "But Surplus Property Disposal Unit Number 437 is famous for overcoming difficulties. Can you be back here at one o'clock with the cash?"

They said they could. We exchanged about a dozen bows and the aliens left. The price? I won't mention it except to say that when Blackie started quoting figures I nearly passed out.

"We can't get away with this," I told Blackie. "It's too much money. They'll raise hell when they find they've been took."

"Nuts," Blackie said. "They've made a fortune with those rare metals they've been peddling here. This much money is just petty larceny to them. They can afford to laugh it off. It'll be a good cheap education for them."

The aliens walked in at one o'clock sharp and Blackie sold them the moon. All of it. Blackie filled out a fistful of impressive looking papers and traded them for a suitcase full of money. He made their deed effective at midnight on the sixteenth so we'd have plenty of time to get to wherever we decided to go.

We congratulated them on their purchase. They thanked us for our courteous service. Blackie got out a bottle and we drank toasts to each other. I sat there with my hands sweating waiting for them to go but they didn't seem to be in any hurry at all. They got out a bottle of their own and proposed another round of toasts.

Finally Sim said, "What doesss thisss mean—Sssurplusss Property Disssposssal Unit?"

Blackie's eyes lit up. "Just what it says," he told him. "We dispose of all kinds of property. Could we interest you in anything else?"

"It isss quite posssssible that we might like sssomething elsssse," Sim said.

Blackie sat there behind the desk drawing dollar signs on a pad of paper while the aliens waited for him to say something. I was too nervous to open my mouth. Nobody could have said what the aliens were thinking. Those faces of theirs are just about the ultimate in deadpans.

"I'm afraid the property is rather scattered," Blackie said.
"It would take a lot of time to show it to you." He was thinking about that date he'd put on the moon deed.

"We would be glad to furnisssh the transssportasssion,"
Sim said.

Which is how Blackie and I got a ride in one of their space
ships. I won't brag about it. I was sick from the minute we took
off. It didn't affect Blackie at all and he spent the trip looking
the ship over. He said afterward that he couldn't make head
nor tail of it.

Our first stop was New York and Blackie started things off
by selling them the Brooklyn Bridge. That took some selling
and Blackie isn't at his best when he can't use both hands when
he talks. He was keeping that suitcase of money clamped
under one arm.

At first the aliens seemed to have trouble figuring out what
the bridge was there for. They made such a commotion looking
it over that they attracted a crowd and a police car stopped to
see what was going on. I was ready to cut and run. Blackie
waved his free hand and explained that the aliens were admir-
ing the bridge—and the police actually gave us an escort to
keep the crowd back!

The aliens finally got it across to us that it was the river
that bothered them. I thought at the time that they were afraid
it would dry up and make the bridge worthless. Right now I
don't know what they thought. Blackie solved the problem in a
hurry by adding ten grand to the purchase price and throwing
in the East River and they snapped it up. They also bought
the Empire State Building. Then we went down to Washington
and sold the Washington Monument. Blackie tried to interest
them in the Capitol Building but they wouldn't have any part
of that.

Blackie wanted to take them around the world and dispose
of Buckingham Palace and the Eiffel Tower and the Taj Mahal
and a lot of other famous things. I said nix and in the end
he agreed with me. What we'd already sold added up to
enough money to last us the rest of our lives. If we sold them

too much it might get the thing out of the petty larceny class and cause a lot of trouble.

So we told them it was quitting time and we'd show them more stuff in the morning. It was late evening when we got back to the office. Blackie gave them another stack of official looking papers and the aliens gave us two more suitcases full of money.

And they were all set to take legal possession of the moon and Brooklyn Bridge along with the East River and the Empire State Building and the Washington Monument at midnight of the sixteenth, Eastern Standard Time. Or so they thought.

"It hasss indeed been a pleasssure," Sim said.

"The pleasure was all ours," Blackie told him.

We had another drink together and another series of bows and they left promising to be back promptly at ten A.M. to continue their shopping tour. We cleared out right after them. Blackie left a nice bonus for our secretary with a note telling her to get rid of the aliens and close the office and we got out of town fast. We sold our car in Minneapolis and bought another one and on the sixteenth—yesterday—we were holed up here in Colorado.

I still couldn't figure out how the aliens could be so stupid. Blackie said they were such morons they didn't even know how to fly their space ships since they'd taken us to New York by way of Mexico City. I said the important thing was that they'd gotten us there and in nothing flat and they had to be smart to do that. Blackie said they'd be a lot smarter at one minute after midnight on the sixteenth and we left it at that.

We were just getting up this morning when we heard the news on the eight o'clock broadcast—how the Brooklyn Bridge and the Empire State Building and the Washington Monument all disappeared last night between midnight and one A.M. The people who were around those places had some odd stories to tell but I don't understand yet how the aliens managed it. Those using the bridge got off and those wanting to use it couldn't get on and then—presto it was gone. Same thing about the buildings. The East River wasn't mentioned so I guess that's still there. Maybe it was a little too much for the aliens or maybe they were satisfied with the water that was under the bridge at the time.

We didn't hear anything about the moon either. Last night it was cloudy around here but it wasn't cloudy everywhere and if the moon is gone someone should have missed it. That's been bothering us. Blackie's hoping that they decided to leave it where it is. My hunch is that they found the bridge and the Empire State Building and the Washington Monument enough work for one night and they're coming back for it later. We'd like to know but we figure it'd be dangerous to start calling the papers and the observatories to ask if the moon is still there.

Right now it's only four in the afternoon and Blackie is already outside waiting for the moon to come up. I sure hope he won't be disappointed.

Sooner or later someone is certain to blame the aliens for this. I hope you won't mind a long honeymoon in Mexico and after that we might even have to go to Brazil.

But you can blow the works on that trousseau. Be seeing you.

Loads of Love from

Spike

3

ON THE DOTTED LINE

1. ERF ZEDDEN

I've been sleeping one off, stretched out nice and comfortable in some shrubbery on a rise that overlooks the Detroit River. It's been a balmy night, and I wake up feeling good and lie there looking around, and—Zip! This fellow comes stumbling out of nowhere, trips, and flops down on top of me.

Out of nowhere, I said. I'm watching, and one second he isn't there and the next second he is. I squirm out from under him and get my breath back and look up to see if maybe he fell out of an aircar. There aren't any aircars, and I tell myself that's the last time I'll ever mix Martian gin with Venusian wine.

He sits up and looks at me, rubbing his eyes, and his jaw works two or three times before he gets any words out. Then when he finally says, "Where am I?" he talks like his mouth is wired shut.

"That's a real easy one," I say. "I'd rather hear about how you got here."

He stands up and takes a few steps, craning his neck and staring in all directions. "Where am I?" he says again.

"New Detroit," I say. "Down by the river, as maybe you've noticed."

He takes another look around and gets mad. "Look," he says. "I know Detroit backward and there isn't any park that looks like this. Where's the Civic Center? And how come I can't see the Penobscot Building? That must be Belle Isle out there, so I should be able to see the center of town from here."

I'm looking him over, trying not to laugh at the way he talks and at the queer clothes he's wearing. He's not a bad-looking fellow, young and well built, but he has his hair cut straight across the top in the weirdest haircut I've ever seen. I'm beginning to wonder if maybe he's a refugee from a police psych board.

"Never heard of those places," I say, "and you're about twenty miles from the center of town."

He sits down again, looking so bewildered I commence feeling sorry for him.

"This is Detroit, Michigan, U.S.A.?"

I tell him that it's New Detroit, and I've heard that New Detroit is in Michigan Province though I don't offer any guarantee. And the letters he mentions don't mean anything to me.

He makes like an enfant trying to get something straightened out. "This is Detroit—"

"New Detroit."

"Michigan—"

"Michigan Province—maybe."

"It's July fifteenth—"

"Something like that," I say. I haven't been keeping a close check on the date.

I decide maybe I'd better get him out of sight until I make up my mind about him. I take his arm and start walking, and he follows along without saying anything.

He keeps looking around, though, like he's never seen New Detroit before. And if he hasn't I can't blame him for looking. It was rough on those cities that got wiped out in the big war, but they had the advantage of a fresh start. New Detroit is a beautiful place—the whole city one big park, with all of the commercial places and ground transportation and a lot of the dwellings underground and just the apartment communities stretching up into the sky at regular intervals.

He looks back at the river. "Are we far from Lake Erie?" he asks.

"Not far. You can see it from an aircar if you go up high enough."

"And Lake St. Clair?"

"You mean Lake Clair. Real close."

"And that's the Detroit River?"

"Never heard it called anything else."

"And this is Detroit?"

"New Detroit."

He takes a deep breath. "What year is this?"

"2337," I say.

So help me, the man passes out.

I signal an aircab, and he comes to a little later and I get him down to my hotel room on the seventh level without any trouble. I drop a coin in the visiscope and leave him in front of the screen watching while I go out to get him some presentable clothes. When I come back he's still sitting there, but he looks primed for an explosion.

"No advertising!" he says.

I ask him what that is.

"Why, advertising. You know—they talk about a product, or sing songs about it, to make people want to buy it."

"Sounds silly," I say. "I never heard of anything like that. I don't think it would work anyway. Singing a song wouldn't make *me* want to buy anything."

"But it does work," he insists. "You see—"

I'm looking him over, trying to decide whether he's serious or stringing me. I don't get to decide because he shrugs and says, "Skip it."

A moment later he starts in again. "This is Detroit?"

"New Detroit."

"And there's no advertising?"

"*I* never heard of any."

"How do things get sold?"

"Why, there are salesmen all over the place. They don't bother me none because I'm a space bug. Our credit isn't worth much. When I want something I go to a merchandise center and pay cash. Now let's get these clothes on you."

I coax him out of the funny outfit he's wearing and then I have a fight on my hands getting him into the new clothes. He doesn't mind the shorts but he raises a big fuss about the cape. "What's the sense in wearing a transparent cape?" he wants to know.

"Everybody wears them on Earth," I say. "I don't care much for them myself, but that's the way things are here. In space we wear practical clothes."

"Everybody—you mean—*women* wear them?"

"Sure," I say and give him a wink. "Some wear more transparent ones than others."

"My name is Mark Jackson," he says slowly. "I'm an automobile salesman—a *good* salesman. I live in Detroit, and the year is 1957, and I want to go home."

"My name is Erf Zedden," I say. "I'm a space bug but probably not a very good one. I work on a Mars-Callisto ore freighter, and I'm on a six-month leave. It's my first time on Earth in over five years, and the year is 2337. And what the hell is an automobile?"

He doesn't answer, so I slap him on the back and tell him I could use a drink and he looks like he could use more than one, so we go up two levels to a bar that's run by an ex-space bug.

This fellow Jackson acts real queer. He keeps staring at the women, and while I must admit that in that bar their capes were more transparent than in most places, I begin to wonder if he's never seen a female before.

"This is 2337?" he says finally.

"Until next January," I say.

"I've been trying to think what could have done it," he says. "There was that fallout from the bomb tests. All the papers were screaming about it, but the scientists said it wasn't dangerous, and it shouldn't have affected me more than anyone else. And then there was that damned X-ray machine—"

He stops to take a long squirt of Martian gin. I wait quietly, thinking that if I don't interrupt him maybe he'll start talking sense.

"I went to sell a car to a doctor," he goes on, "and while I was waiting to see him I leaned against the X-ray machine, and somehow the damned thing got turned on. The doctor said it was only a few seconds and nothing to worry about. There probably were other things—it was that kind of day. And then the automobile accident wrapped it up. I was driving away from the doctor's office, and this kid ran smack out in front of me. The top was down on my convertible. When I swerved I hit a utility pole and it threw me over the fence into a Detroit Edison Company transformer. I just had time to think, 'This is it, fellow!' and then here I was. 2337, you say?"

"Until next January."

He takes another man-sized drink of gin. "I don't believe it."

I tell him he'll forget his troubles if we pick up a couple of girls, but he says no, he wants to think things over. So we go back to my hotel room, and the place is jammed with police. Someone saw me bringing him in and reported it. They take the two of us, and all those queer clothes of his, to Police Central, and it takes me two days to convince them that I don't know anything about him. When I leave they won't tell me what they've done with him, so naturally I figure they're holding him for psych-conditioning.

Well—I know I did the best I could for him. My leave still has four months to run, and I have money left, so I take the next rocket to New York.

2. PROFESSOR JOHN PARKINS

It was early August of 2337 when I received a telememo from my old friend Bran Crustin, Police Commissioner of the Michigan Province. The case that he described to me was psychologically routine, but it did have its intriguing aspects. I was, of course, happy to be of any possible assistance. There was no Boston-New Detroit rocket service at that time, so I took the shuttle to New York, where I caught the New Detroit rocket.

I spent three days in studying the various artifacts that the alleged man-from-the-past claimed to have brought with him and in listening to recordings of the various interviews that he'd had. I also discussed his case in detail with the doctors in charge before I asked to see him.

Four husky attendants brought him into the room. It was obvious that they considered him violent, though he looked rational enough. His face was young and good-looking, in spite of its sullenness. His physique was impressive. He appeared to be a leader, a man accustomed to dominating.

"I don't recognize you," he said angrily. "What's your specialty? Lie detector tests? Sanity tests?"

He took a step forward, and the attendants leaped to restrain him. I waved them off and dismissed them. I had already decided that this Mark Jackson, whatever else he might be, was not insane. I felt confident that he would not be violent if I treated him civilly.

"Sit down, please," I said.

We sat facing each other across a table where Jackson's personal effects and odd clothing were spread out. "I'm John Parkins," I told him. "Professor of American History at Harvard University. I've been studying your property and listening to recordings of the interviews you've had."

"And like everyone else, you think I'm nuts!" he snapped.

I stared at him. "What a quaint way to put it! But no, I don't doubt your sanity. And I am absolutely convinced as to the genuineness of your property. These are unquestionably twentieth century artifacts. The monetary value would not be tremendous, but a number of museums would be delighted to have them. Further, in its verifiable portions your knowledge of the twentieth century is completely accurate. Even your accent and speech are authentic, at least according to current theory."

He jumped to his feet and paced back and forth for a moment. "That's a switch. Being believed, I mean. Does it mean that I get out of here?"

"Switch—" I murmured. Everything the man said was convincing, but I could not allow myself to be convinced. A historian deals confidently with records, documents, artifacts, but he cannot be so rash as to enter a judgement as to the historical authenticity of a living human being! "No," I said. "It doesn't mean that you can be released."

"Oh, great. You believe me, and now I suppose they have you in here with me!"

I smiled. "No. I asked to see you so I could give you some advice. The doctors are determined to cure you of your delusions. Let them cure you."

"How?"

"They think you're a history student who's suffered some kind of traumatic amnesia and gotten his studies mixed up with reality. Agree with them, and they'll probably let you go."

"How can I agree with them when I know they're wrong?"

"Agree with them," I said firmly. "You've upset the authorities enough already. The mere fact that your fingerprints are not registered anywhere has caused panic in four branches of the government. Don't disturb them further. Just do what you're told and believe what you're told, and eventually you'll be released."

"Do you believe me?"

"I believe that you have an amazing knowledge of the twentieth century, however you acquired it. It shouldn't be wasted. Come to me when you're released, and I'll arrange a teaching position for you. You should make an excellent historian."

"No, thank you," Jackson said. "I'm a salesman—a *good* salesman. Teaching wouldn't interest me."

"At least give it careful consideration. And remember—the sooner you co-operate, the sooner you'll be released."

After I returned to Boston, I continued to give considerable thought to this Mark Jackson, for a more perplexing problem has not come to my attention in all of my years of scholarly investigation. Finally I wrote to Arnold Stephens, a cousin of my wife, who is personnel manager of the Terra Sales Corporation. I outlined what I believed to be the facts in the Jackson case and asked him if he would be able to give the young man assistance in establishing himself.

He answered that he would be happy to interview him, but that he could promise no more consideration than would be extended to any other applicant for a sales position. I immediately contacted the New Detroit police. Jackson had already been certified cured and released, and they did not know where he had gone. I gathered that they were only too pleased to have him off their hands.

3. ARNOLD STEPHENS

Mark Jackson came to the offices of Terra Sales Corporation only a few days after I received Professor Parkins' letter concerning him. I recognized his name immediately, of course, and assumed that the professor had sent him.

For many years I have interviewed all sales applicants myself, as I am considered an excellent subject for this task. I had Jackson brought to me at once, and after what Parkins had written I was rather surprised to find nothing obviously different about him. The odd inflection in his speech I could have overlooked, and otherwise he seemed quite normal. If I had not known Parkins so well, personally and professionally, I might have considered myself the victim of a joke. Jackson was a good-looking young man, rather more solemn than most, and the only thing that set him apart from the other applicants I'd interviewed that morning was his attitude of quiet determination.

"I suppose you know that Professor Parkins wrote to me about you," I said.

He looked surprised. "Why, no. I talked with a gentleman of

that name three or four weeks ago, but we discussed—other things."

"I see. Why do you want to be a salesman?"

He jumped to his feet. "I *am* a salesman," he said firmly. And he started in. Never have I witnessed such an amazing performance. He handled himself with the skill of a trained elocutionist. He was more than eloquent—he was brilliantly persuasive. Had it not been for his accent and his frequent use of strange words, I might have been carried away. Much of his discourse concerned his skill and experience in selling automobiles, which I later found to be an obsolete type of conveyance.

It was remarkable, and it was also pitiful. I heard him out to the end and shook my head sadly. "Sorry," I said. "I can't use you."

"Why not?" he demanded.

Salesman qualifications were then the most carefully guarded secret in the business world. Though I couldn't give him a direct answer, I felt that his performance entitled him to more than the usual curt dismissal. "Have you applied at any other sales corporation?" I asked.

"Hell, yes! This is the twenty-third, and I have sixteen to go. I started with manufacturers. Nothing doing. None of them have any salesmen. The Cadrovet Aircar Company in New Detroit offered me any one of five different jobs, but it wouldn't hire me as a salesman. They told me it's been a hundred and fifty years since they used their own salesmen. All selling is done by sales corporations. So I came to New York to try the sales corporations, and they all told me the same thing. 'Young man, to be a salesman you must first be able to sell yourself.' That's sensible, so I rented a recorder. Last night I was up most of the night working on a sales talk to sell myself. You just heard it. I think it's good. Damn it, I *know* it's good! But I still get the same story. Sell yourself. At my last call a fat old geezer leered at me and said, 'Make me hire you. I dare you!'"

I chuckled. "That would be Barlow, of Sales Unlimited."

"Look. I *know* I can sell. All I want is a chance. You can hire me on a commission basis, and it won't cost you a thing if I don't deliver. What's wrong with that? Am I poison or something?"

"Professor Parkins said that you think you were transferred somehow from the twentieth century. He seems halfway inclined to believe you."

Jackson gestured disgustedly. "I'm not admitting anything. I spent enough time in that hospital."

"I understand," I said. "But even if you were a good salesman in—well, somewhere else—I'm afraid you'll have to find some other way to make a living. I'd advise you to take one of those jobs at Cadrovet."

"All I want is a chance," he pleaded. "I know what I can do. I can sell anything."

"To everyone?" I asked.

"What do you mean?"

I thought for a moment. "Because of your unusual background I'm going to make an exception and show you what is required of our salesman. Follow me, please."

I took him to the records room and pulled a file at random. "Here's last week's record of one of our salesmen. He's only a marginal worker, but he's improving. You can see that he made a hundred and seven sales contacts, or about twenty-one a day. From those contacts he made two hundred and forty sales, of which twenty-two were majors—sales amounting to two thousand dollars or more."

"Didn't anyone say no?" Jackson exclaimed.

"Of course not," I said. "We have no use for a salesman to whom people can say no. I don't know what your record may have been back in the—elsewhere—but unless you can do almost as well as this, no sales corporation could afford to waste time with you. And you couldn't afford to waste your time. This salesman is earning a living, though not a very good one. If he doesn't show a substantial improvement by the end of the year, we'll either discharge him or transfer him."

"I see," Jackson said. Suddenly he looked terribly weary.

"Better go back to Cadrovet," I told him. "They're a good company, and they must think you have ability or they wouldn't have offered you your choice of five jobs."

"They gave me aptitude tests for two days. But I'm a salesman. I wouldn't be happy sitting behind a desk or tinkering with an assembly line. I'm grateful to you for being decent to me, but I can't take your advice."

"I gather that your finances are limited. You'll have to work at something."

"I know. Well—this morning I ran into a fellow I met in New Detroit. Erf Zedden. He's a space bug, and he thinks he can get me a job on a Mars-Callisto ore freighter. Right now that sounds pretty good."

"That's no place for a man with ability," I said.

"I suppose not, but I feel like getting away from things. I need time to think."

I talked with him for a few minutes longer, trying to cheer him up, but without much success. He thanked me and left, and it was more than two years before I saw him again.

4. ERF ZEDDEN

I run into this Mark Jackson again in New York, and he looks so miserable I'm afraid he's about to jump in the river. My money is running out, and he tells me the money he got from selling some of his stuff to a museum is running out, and I say, "What the hell! I'm going back to Mars in a couple of days. Come down to the Jovian Mining Company's office with me and I'll get you a job. The Mars-Callisto run is an easy one, the pay is good, and when you're too old to push the ore they retire you on a good pension. What can you lose?"

He says he'll think it over, but he has a few more people he wants to see. Later that day he comes to my hotel and says, "When do we leave?" So we're off for Mars.

Believe me, this Jackson is a good man. Two months on the job, and he's my boss. At the end of a year he's running the whole show at the Callisto end, and the Jovian Mining Company gives me a bonus for recruiting him. Never saw a fellow go up so fast, but somehow he doesn't seem happy about it. No matter how high he goes, though, we're still good friends, and whenever I hit Callisto I stay with him.

So it's natural when I start talking about a leave on Earth he thinks he could use a vacation himself, and we make arrangements to go together and do the old planet up good.

I get to Earth first, because he insists on stopping off for a tourist's tour of the moon. I say, "What's so special about Earth's moon when you been living on one of Jupiter's moons for nearly two years?" But he won't listen, so I get to Stellar City a day ahead of him. I find a room for us at a spacers' hostel, and the next morning I leave a note for him to meet me at the Rocket Club and go out to line up a couple of girls. And that's the day things really start jumping on Earth.

These girls I pick up are some characters—tall, hefty creatures with capes so transparent they might as well not wear any. They have their hair strung up in one of these gravity-defying styles, and they look like they're nuclear propelled. I'm thinking this is one leave that's going to be worth remembering.

We sit around the Rocket Club having a few drinks, and a little later Jackson comes in, and we start back up Pluto Boulevard toward the hostel. And all of a sudden this mob comes charging down on us.

Like I said, this is the day things start jumping on Earth. We back up against a building as the mob tears past, and we get a quick look at the chalky face of the man they're chasing. He's running for his life, and the mob is the most hate-twisted bunch of murderers I've ever seen.

"Good riddance," one of the girls says. "Let's watch them finish him off."

Jackson hasn't heard what's going on, and he yelps, "Hey! What's this all about?"

There isn't time to answer him. The mob gallops past, and I manage to hail an aircab, and we climb aboard and drift along with the small fleet that's hovering above to watch the show.

"Why are they chasing him?" Jackson asks.

"He's a hypno," I tell him.

He's a pretty fair hypnotist, and he makes it a good show. He glances over his shoulder now and then, and freezes two or three of the mob. The others just bowl them over and trample on them and keep on going. Off in the distance I spot some air patrol units coming in at top speed, and I wonder if they'll make it in time.

They don't, of course. The hypno runs as long as he can, and then he turns to face the mob. Even a Grade I hypno wouldn't have stood a chance. All the mob has to do is avoid his eyes. It climbs all over him, knives flash, and by the time the patrols land the mob has scattered and there's nothing left for them to do but clean up the mess.

The cab drops us at the hostel. The girls are still squealing excitedly, and Jackson looks sick. We go up to our room, and he drops into a chair and takes a good gulp of Martian gin out of a bottle.

"Why?" he says.

"Why what?" one of the girls says.

"Why did they murder that man?"

The girl stares at him. "Haven't you heard?"

"I haven't heard anything. I just got in from the moon a couple of hours ago—remember?"

I go over and drop a coin in the visiscope, and we settle down to watch. Paris. Six hundred hypnotists murdered and the total rising. Shots of mobs chasing hypnos. Applause and snickers from the girls. London. More than two hundred hypnos murdered. Uncontrolled mobs chasing about the streets. The International Institute of Hypnology in flames. New York. Martial Law declared. No estimate of casualties available. And so it goes.

"The congressional committee released its report this morning," one of the girls says. "Millions of hypnotists on Earth, and eighty-five per cent of them are salesmen. Every time you turn around one of them sells you something, and you wonder why you bought it until the next one sells you something. I came here from Venus three months ago. Know how many aircars I've got? Three. I haven't even got use for one, but I've got three. Bought the last one a week ago, along with a two-year lease on a garage a mile and a half from my apartment. Did I trade in one of the two I already have? No. So I keep asking myself, 'Why? Why do such a stupid thing?' Then this report comes out this morning, and I know. Hypnos sold them to me. I've got two food synthesizers in my apartment. One of them will feed ten people, and I live by myself—most of the time. Lousy hypnos. I've got enough clothes to last me for ten years. I've got a visiscope in every room. There's so much junk in the place I have trouble getting in and out. I came to Earth with plenty of money, and after three months it's all gone and I'll be paying for this stuff for the next twenty years. Hypnos!" She hisses like one of them snakes I see in the zoo the last time I'm on Earth.

"My sister has three carpets on the floor," the other girl says. "Expensive carpets, one right on top of the other. She'd have had a rough time with her husband if he hadn't bought four aircars."

The visiscope keeps switching from city to city. The crisis is planet-wide, and from Moscow to Honolulu hypnos are being chased through the streets or smoked out of their homes.

"I'll tell you one thing," one of the girls says. "When this is over with, the hypnos—if there are any left—won't be selling anything. If the government won't put a stop to it, we'll have ourselves a new government."

Jackson slaps his hands together, kisses both of the girls, and pounds me on the back. I notice a funny look in his eyes that I never see there before. "And I'll have myself a job as a salesman," he says. "Drink, anyone?"

The next morning we throw out the girls and take a rocket to New York. The girls aren't very happy about it. They're looking forward to a month, maybe, with well-charged and well-heeled space men, but we throw them out. Jackson loads up with news strips before we board the rocket, and he keeps his nose in them all the way to New York, reading about the riots.

I do some reading myself, just to pass the time, and I don't see anything very exciting about that congressional report. It just says that hypnos make up a bigger hunk of the population than they'd thought, and it gives a breakdown on the occupations of hypnos: two per cent politicians, eight per cent working in some branch of medicine, three per cent criminals, two per cent in various other things, and eighty-five per cent salesmen.

This doesn't mean much to us space bugs. Salesmen have never bothered us because we don't have credit ratings. But the rest of the population is in debt up to its ears from buying, buying—things it doesn't need and can't afford. When the report comes out people start putting two and two together, and they don't like the answer.

In New York Jackson drags me along with him to a fancy office building. The sign above the door says TERRA SALES CORPORATION, and inside everything is a mess. There are police on guard, men are replacing broken windows and sweeping up debris in the big lobby, and all the employees are looking like a rich uncle has just died intestate.

Jackson seems real happy about everything, and he talks his way past the guards and the secretaries, and we end up in the office of a man named Stephens.

He greets us very politely, though it's obvious that he's in no mood to talk to us or anyone else. "I remember you," he says to Jackson. "You're the man from—how are you getting along?"

Jackson pulls up a couple of chairs, and we sit down, and Jackson leans across the desk like it belongs to him instead of this Stephens. After seeing him operate on Callisto, I wonder if maybe he's going to take over this place.

"I understand, now, why you wouldn't hire me," Jackson says. "All of your salesmen are hypnotists."

Stephens nods. "Of course."

"And if a man couldn't hypnotize you into hiring him, you turned him down."

Stephens nods again. "I have more than a normal resistance to hypnosis, and if a man can hypnotize me, I know he's good. Of course we wouldn't hire just *any* hypnotist."

"According to today's news strips, the government will take action before the day is out to prevent you from hiring any hypnotists at all. So I want a job."

"The answer is still no," Stephens says.

"If hypnotists can't sell for you, you'll have to hire someone else or go out of business."

"We had a policy meeting this morning," Stephens says. "The General Council of Sales Companies also had a meeting. We've agreed to go out of business, if it comes to that." He grins at us, but it isn't the happy kind of grin. "Any restrictions the government imposes can't last more than a month. That'll be long enough to produce the worst business slump in history. Our economy simply can't function without the hypnotists. There's no other way to make the population consume our enormous output of material goods. I'm sorry, but the recommendation I gave you two years ago still stands."

"I think you're out of touch with the situation," Jackson says. "These restrictions aren't going to be temporary. I've waited more than two years, though, so I guess I can wait a little longer."

Stephens tells him, friendly like, that he'll be wasting his time, and we shake hands with him and leave.

"What happens now?" I ask.

"We ask the Jovian Mining Company for an indefinite leave of absence," Jackson says. "Then we get jobs—something in the government service, I think, where this slump won't hit us. And we wait. I'm going to get a job as a salesman. Maybe I'll even make a salesman out of you!"

I don't think much of that idea. I like this fellow, though, so I go along with him. We don't have any trouble about leaves of absence. I've been with the company eighteen years, and I have a lot of accumulated leave time. And Jackson is such

a good man that they want him back. So we get jobs with the
postal service and wait to see what will happen.

5. ARNOLD STEPHENS

At the time Mark Jackson came to see me, we actually thought
we could hold out long enough to get our hypnotists back to
work. The slump developed rapidly. Overnight our economy
changed from one in which everyone bought everything to
one in which no one bought anything. Millions of workers were
unemployed by the end of the second week, and the number
increased daily. The unemployed bought nothing; their re-
serve funds went for indebtedness retirement except for the
ten per cent shelter allowance, and that was absorbed by rent-
als. They seemed perfectly content to forego such luxuries as
fresh food and make use of their past purchases. The average
family owned one food synthesizer per person and could have
subsisted on synthesized food for a year or more without a
single recharge. Those fortunate enough to remain employed
made grudging payments on the things they'd already bought
and tried to save a little money.

All of our predictions came true except one: with the economy in a catastrophic condition, congress still refused to re-
peal its anti-hypno laws. Not until the third month were we
able to persuade a congressman to introduce new legislation,
and he withdrew it the next day when his constituents
started circulating recall petitions.

It was then that we accepted the inevitable and began hiring non-hypnos as salesmen. I made an effort to locate Jackson, but he hadn't left an address, and the mining company
he'd been working for knew nothing about him except that
he was on leave.

He came to see me a month later. "So you're finally hiring
non-hypnos," he said.

"Yes," I admitted.

"One tried to sell me an aircar today. Most miserable performance I've ever seen. He stopped me on the street and hemmed and hawed for at least five minutes and finally said, 'I suppose you wouldn't want to buy a new aircar.' I said no, and he thanked me kindly and walked away."

He laughed uproariously, and there wasn't much that I could say.

"And look here," he said, and waved a news strip under my nose.

In a small box set in the middle of the page a headline ordered me to look at my shoes. I didn't and read on. "Looking shabby? Worn out? Buy a glimmering new pair of EX-CONS!"

"What the devil is that?" I exclaimed.

"Advertisement," he said. "First twenty-fourth-century advertisement I've ever seen. Not bad, either, for an infant profession. Hell of a lot better job than that salesman did."

I pulled out the sales chart for the past four weeks and pushed it across my desk. Jackson stared at it. "No sales?"

"Not one. We've had a thousand non-hypnos out selling, and they haven't made one sale. People are so delighted to be able to say no that they just aren't buying anything. Do you think you could do something about that?"

"You're darned right I could!"

Desperate as our situation was, I hesitated. He was such a likable person that I was reluctant to see him fail. "I'm sure that in a society where there is no hypnotic selling the salesmen will develop highly specialized and efficient techniques," I said, "but I'm frankly dubious that those techniques can succeed in a society where all selling has been hypnotic. I'll give you your opportunity and every possible assistance. I only hope that you won't be too disappointed with the results. I'll take you down to the warehouse, and you can pick out anything you want to sell."

He grinned. "I've been waiting a long time for this. Let's go!"

He selected a stunning household ornament—a miniature portable fountain that contained its own power supply and furnished a dazzling display of color at the touch of a button. I explained the use of our order forms, and he asked for a pocket recorder to take along with him.

"Do you mind if I watch you work?" I asked.

I think the idea pleased him. He spent some time in selecting an apartment building, and when he'd made his choice I asked him why that particular one.

"Government workers," he said. "They're still employed, but they're not in such a high income class that the doors have viewing screens. If you want to sell to a housewife, you have to be able to get your foot in the door."

He started his first call before I could ask him to explain that. As the door opened he made a sweeping bow and announced, "We're making a consumer survey. May we come in?"

I don't know which of us was the more astonished, myself or that plump housewife. She backed away dumbly and allowed us to enter.

I remained by the door while he circled about the living room scrutinizing the furnishings. The housewife trailed after him, looking more bewildered with every step she took.

"The furniture is in fair condition," he remarked. "But you're rather cramped for space, aren't you?"

She stammered, "Why, no—"

"This color scheme clashes badly. Did you select it yourself?"

"Why, I—"

"And the room arrangement. All wrong. I'm sorry, but I'm afraid you can't qualify."

"Qualify for what?" she asked.

Jackson pulled the fountain from his satchel, set it on the table, and touched the button. The room sparkled with color. I looked at the childish delight in that housewife's face and thought, "He's really going to do it!" And the next moment he completely dumbfounded me.

"I've been authorized to place a limited number of these

wonderful fountains in deserving homes," he said. "But as I told you, yours can't qualify. Sorry."

He turned off the fountain, tucked it into the satchel, and started for the door.

I've rarely seen a woman get so angry. Face flushed, arms waving, she planted herself in the doorway and refused to let him go. They argued for a few minutes, and finally he relented and allowed her to sign an order form.

There were sixty-two apartments in that building. Jackson sold sixty-two fountains without varying his technique by one syllable. Then he handed over the order forms and said apologetically, "I'm afraid I'm out of condition. Tired. I'll have to call it a day."

I was exhausted from watching him and reluctant to believe what I'd seen. I kept asking myself, "Is *that* how they sold things in the twentieth century? By insulting the customer and trying to keep him from buying?" I went home myself and went to bed early.

Jackson's call awakened me shortly after midnight. "Better come down to Police Central," he said. "I'm under arrest."

"*Arrest?*" I exclaimed. "How—what—"

"Hypnotic selling," he said. "Twenty-one husbands are down here complaining that I hypnotized their wives into buying those fountains. They tell me the maximum penalty is life imprisonment. I'm surprised it isn't death."

At that moment I had a flicker of doubt—his odd performances, I suppose, and the peculiar reactions of those women. "Jackson," I said, "you didn't by chance hypnotize those women, did you?"

"Certainly not!" he bellowed.

"I'll be right down," I said.

I contacted the firm's legal adviser, and we went together.

Police Central was in an uproar. There were more than forty complaining husbands by the time we got there, and they kept coming in. Some brought their wives with them. The men ranted angrily. The women confessed that Jackson hadn't sold them anything. In fact, he'd tried not to sell them. They'd bought because they wanted the fountain. They still wanted it. A hastily summoned panel of justices heard the evidence, listened to a playback of several sales interviews on Jackson's pocket recorder, and cautiously ventured an opinion that while a hypnotist *might* have riled his potential customers in that manner, they couldn't understand why he would bother. A psychiatrist pronounced Jackson no hypnotist but an extremely shrewd psychologist and perhaps much more dangerous. Reporters gleefully took notes and photographs and interviewed the women. And of course Jackson was released.

The next morning his photo was on visiscope and at the top of every news strip. "Master Salesman," the caption called him. Jackson stormed into my office and said angrily, "We've got to put a stop to this!"

"You're news," I told him. "Except for absolute necessities, that was the first time in months that anyone has bought anything—*on the entire planet!* We can't keep the news media from talking about that."

"I don't like it," he said. He shrugged. "Coming along today?"

He went down to the warehouse and took his own color photos of the latest model aircars, and we flew to the nearest government parking lot. A somewhat battered vehicle came gliding in, and Jackson approached the driver—a portly, important-looking government official.

"Do you own this junk heap?" Jackson asked.

The man winced. "Say—where have I seen you before?"

Jackson ignored the question. "I'm surprised to see a man in your position flying a beat-up job like this. Now look at that car over there." He pointed to a shining model that obviously had been purchased just before the riots. "People judge a man by the car he flies. I'll bet the owner's neighbors think he's *somebody.*"

The man's face modulated through several stages of perplexity. "I never thought of that," he said. "Kids really wear out a car in a hurry. I have five aircars, and every one of them is a mess."

"That's easily solved," Jackson said. "Buy a new car and keep it for yourself." He held up one of his photos. "Really beautiful, isn't it?"

"It certainly is," the man admitted.

Suddenly Jackson had an order form in his hand. "Sign here," he said, "and I'll have it delivered to you this afternoon."

The man signed. I watched Jackson sell seven aircars before I returned to my office. When he reported back early that afternoon, he had thirty-nine signed orders.

Thirty-nine majors! No hypno-salesman had ever been able to extend control over that many qualified customers in one day. "Amazing!" I said. "Are you certain you don't have some kind of latent hypnotic ability?"

"If I did, I wouldn't be a salesman," he said. "Where's the pleasure in selling if the customer can't say no?"

"Whatever it is, I'm convinced. I've never been more resoundingly convinced in my life. I'm going to ask the board to make you vice-president in charge of sales training. If you can teach other men to do what you're doing—"

"Not yet," he said. "I need to experiment. There's something about this that bothers me. The people are too naïve. With the childish approaches I'm using I should get a lot of refusals, and I don't. Tomorrow I'm going to try fountains again."

Jackson was in the news again the next morning, and so were the men who'd bought aircars from him. Some of them were chagrined, some angry, one or two thought they'd needed a new aircar.

"I wish they'd quit that," Jackson said.

"They won't," I told him. "You're news, and the people who buy from you are news. You might as well get used to it."

He picked up a fountain at the warehouse and started on his calls. The first housewife met us at the door with a long stare, followed by a squeal of delight. "You're the *salesman!* I saw your picture! Do come in!"

Jackson glared at me, shrugged disgustedly, and then fixed a smile on his face for the benefit of the housewife. We followed her into the living room, and she hovered about him excitedly.

"I read all about it," she gushed. "Do it to me, just like you did to all those other women."

Jackson was holding his smile with difficulty. He glanced at the room. "No. I'm sorry. I'm afraid you can't qualify—"

She shrieked with laughter. "That's it!" she giggled. "That's exactly it. I read all about it. Do it some more!"

"Your living room is much too small."

Another giggle. "That's it!"

"The color scheme clashes badly."

"That's it!"

He placed the fountain on the table. "It's a beautiful ornament, but I'm afraid you can't qualify."

"That's all right," she said. "My husband wouldn't want me to buy it. But thank you ever so much for showing it to me."

We found ourselves in the hallway again, both of us thoroughly unnerved. We had ten more sessions with fascinated, giggling housewives before Jackson gave up and went home. He sold no fountains.

The next morning he switched to aircars again, and he was back before noon—with no orders.

"They slap me on the back," he said. "They offer to buy me drinks. I had more free drinks pushed at me this morning than in any six months I can remember. They take me around and introduce me to their friends. And when I try to point their thinking toward a sale, they laugh in my face and say, 'So you're the salesman! Sell me something!'"

"The publicity," I said.

"Yes. I'll have to think of something new."

He did. The next day he was sensational. The following day he failed to make a single sale. As the days passed that pattern was repeated again and again. He would try out a new approach and enjoy phenomenal success. Invariably an army of reporters would pick up the names of his customers at Credit Central and interview them, and the next morning all of the details would be dramatically unveiled to the reading and listening public. And that particular approach never worked again.

"I think I understand it," he said finally. "If I catch this twenty-fourth century customer unawares, he's incredibly naïve. He can't say no. But if he's forewarned, he has a terrific sales resistance. If we could only get rid of the publicity—"

"We can't," I said. "The question is, could you teach other salesmen to come up with new approaches every day?"

"No. In time some of them could, but it takes native ability and lots of selling experience. All I could do at the start would be to teach them an approach I've tested myself."

"But once you've tested it, it won't work again."

"That seems to be true."

"Then I'm afraid we're beaten," I said. "You're making a remarkable record, but one man can't stop an economic slump all by himself."

Jackson got to his feet wearily. "There must be some way to lick the problem. And if there is, I'll find it."

But he didn't find it. He worked incessantly, his face took on a haunted expression, and he grew increasingly irritable. He seemed to be wearing himself away, day by day, and finally I made him take a week's rest.

During that week congress took courage and acted. It drew up a detailed code of what could be sold to whom, and how much, and let the hypnos go back to work. When Jackson returned, the economic slump was on its way out. Much as I regretted it, so was Jackson.

"You can have your job back and carry on any way you like," I told him. "I appreciate what you tried to do, and no one denies that your performance was remarkable. You'd have a difficult time competing with hypnos, though."

He took it amazingly well. "I know I would," he said grimly. "But I still think I can lick this problem. I'll keep working on it. And I promise you—I'll be back."

I never expected to see him again.

6. ERF ZEDDEN

Jackson gives me a bad time while he's being a salesman, and it gets worse by the day. He climbs all over me if some little thing goes wrong around the apartment, and he sits up most of the night figuring out ways to sell things. I think the fellow is killing himself, and I'm damned glad when his boss makes him take a week off. We go to one of those luxury hotels on the moon for the whole week, and though I hate the place I don't say anything, because I figure he needs the rest.

The day after we get back to Earth he goes to work as usual and comes home a little later to tell me the whole thing is off. I consider this the first good news since the riots. We leave for Mars the same day, and the Jovian Mining Company is glad to have us back—him, anyway. They make him take a demotion for being away so long, but in no time at all he's back where he was, and he keeps going up. It takes him just five years to make it all the way to president.

We go to live on Mars, and I get a promotion and a raise in salary to be what he calls his right-hand man, which mostly consists of seeing that he stays healthy and running errands for him. He keeps me worried because no matter how high he goes, I can see he isn't happy. As he says to me maybe ten thousand times, "Once a salesman, always a salesman." That's what he wants to be, and he's convinced himself he's going back, some day, and show all those hypnos how it's done.

He paces the floor with that funny look in his eyes, and sometimes he's up late at night thinking of ways to sell things and making up sales talks. He practices the sales talks on me, and I keep telling him they're good, though after I hear one or two they all sound pretty much the same.

Things go on that way for a couple of years, with me getting more and more worried about Jackson's health, and then a sudden development in the mining business gives him something else to think about. The mines on Callisto start paying out.

Now, the Jovian Mining Company expects this for the last fifty years, and new operations are underway on Ganymede and Europa and Io long before I first hit space, and the company makes maybe ten million per cent profit on its Callisto investment, and nobody feels bad about pulling out.

Nobody except Jackson. *He* thinks it's a crisis, and he drags me off to a directors meeting to run a projector for him.

"It's a scandalous waste," he says. "We have six good-sized towns on Callisto, and the cost of salvaging that fused plastic would be more than it's worth."

"Don't give it a thought," they tell him. "If it costs too much to salvage, just forget about it."

"It isn't good business to write off an investment of that size."

"My dear fellow," they say. "Our investment on Callisto was amortized a hundred years ago. The company never thought the mines would produce this long. It's excellent business to write it off."

Jackson shakes his head, and I see that funny look in his eyes. "Callisto is the sole property of the Jovian Mining Company," he says. "It's no longer of any use to us, so I'm asking the board of directors for permission to sell it."

There's about two minutes of silence, followed by the wildest laughter I've heard since the anti-hypno riots. Those old men just lean back and laugh themselves silly. Sell Callisto? Why not sell Mars? Or Earth?

Jackson waits calmly until they quiet down, and then he puts it in the form of a motion, Callisto to be sold, with the company retaining all mineral rights. The directors can't see anything wrong with the idea except that it isn't possible, and Jackson gets unanimous approval. The next morning we leave for Earth.

Jackson rents a reference machine, and he spends a few days filling a ledger with notes and statistics and a few more days getting these organized. Then we call on a Mr. Whaley, who is president of a large travel bureau.

"I understand you people have had a tough time since that

legislation on hypnotic selling went into effect," Jackson says. This Mr. Whaley is glad to have a shoulder to cry on, and he tells us his troubles. Before the anti-hypno riots he has hypno salesmen out selling travel tours to people who don't want them. A lot of people don't even want them after they buy them, so they don't use the tickets, which adds up to a nice slice of pure profit for the travel agency. After the riots, the government puts a stop to this.

"Ever since then, you've been looking for outstanding attractions to make people want to travel," Jackson says.

"We have," Whaley admits.

"And right now you're thinking of building a luxury Honeymoon Hotel on the moon."

"We *were* thinking about it," Whaley says. "The hotels already there would provide stiff competition, and construction costs have been rising so fast that we'd have to charge rates that young couples couldn't afford."

"I have the answer to your problem," Jackson says. "Take your honeymooners to Callisto, where excellent accommodations are already built. You'd have to make a few alterations, but the expense would be minor."

"It's too far," Whaley says. "Most of the honeymoons would have to be over before the young people could get there."

"I believe I have some facts that would interest you," Jackson says, and he opens his ledger.

He tosses statistics at Whaley for twenty minutes. He shows him that ninety per cent of the immigrants to Mars are young and unmarried and what the Martian marriage rate is. He shows him how much money the government is spending to interest the citizens of Earth in settling elsewhere in the solar system and how the government would joyfully furnish subsidies for a Callisto honeymoon fleet equipped with fast military drives. "The high marriage rate on Mars assures you of a stable business right from the start that will more than carry your operating costs," he says. "You can play Earth and the rest of the solar system for the super luxury trade. What's more, you'll have something to sell. Something that will in-

terest and excite people. Think of the slogans you can use—
'Honeymoon among the moons—the sixteen moons of Jupiter.
Honeymoon under Jupiter, the biggest moon in the universe.'
Man, it's a natural!"

Whaley shakes the dreamy look out of his eyes and says,
"Just what are *you* trying to sell?"

"Callisto," Jackson says.

"We aren't big enough. No travel agency is big enough."

"All the agencies together are big enough," Jackson says. "All
of you can profit. This is a plan to *create* business."

"I have no authority," Whaley says. "I'd have to take it up
with the council."

"Just introduce me," Jackson says, "and I'll take it up with
the council."

It ends, of course, with his selling Callisto. At least, he sells
the Jovian Mining Company's surface holdings on Callisto, but
to the news services it amounts to the same thing. For a few
days we're overrun with reporters and Jackson gets a big
play in the headlines—MASTER SALESMAN SELLS MOON,
and that sort of thing. The directors of the Jovian Mining
Company send Jackson a bonus and vote him a chunk of stock
and tell him as long as he's already on Earth he should take a
vacation. I'm afraid he'll get ideas about being a salesman
again, but he doesn't. He just takes a vacation.

Then one day this man Stephens, of Terra Sales Corporation,
invites us to have dinner with him. I think maybe he wants
Jackson to come back to work, but no, we just have a good
dinner, and Jackson meets his daughter, and from the way they
react on each other I think Jackson will be in the market for one
of those Callisto honeymoons.

"I see that you've solved your problem," Stephens says.

"Yes," Jackson says. "I've solved it. If my sales presentations
won't work more than once, all I have to do is sell something
that only needs to be sold once."

At the time I don't understand this, but right now I'm giving
it some thought. Jackson marries the Stephens girl and brings
her back to Mars, where he settles down to raise a big family

and increase the profits of the Jovian Mining Company. He's a cinch to be the next chairman of the board, which is a neat achievement for a young man, but I can see he's still not satisfied with himself.

The trouble is, Callisto doesn't really solve his problem. He can't be happy unless he's selling something, and even I can see that a man who sells things that can only be sold once is going to spend a lot of time out of work. As Jackson admits himself, the supply of moons is even more limited than the demand.

Lately I see that funny look in his eyes, and it bothers me to see him looking that way when there isn't anything for him to sell. I think maybe this has something to do with the amount of time he spends studying an old book that he pays an antique dealer a small fortune for back on Earth. It's called *Hypnotism Self-Taught.*

4

JUDGEMENT DAY

Lem Dyer was used to being talked about. For years people had thought him a bit touched in the head, or a harmless dreamer, or maybe some kind of soothsayer, and in Glenn Center when folks thought something they said it. Lem never minded.

They were saying other things about him that evening, foul, vicious things. Lem heard some of them, spewed up from the crowd that gathered below his cell window. He tilted the battered old chair back against the cement-block wall and sat there in the dark, puffing slowly on his corncob pipe and only half listening to the arguments, and the coarse shouts, and the jeers. "Shucks," he told himself. "They don't mean nothin' by it."

And after a while he heard the sheriff's booming voice talking to the crowd, telling the men to go home, telling them they had nothing to worry about, and they might as well leave Lem Dyer alone with his conscience.

"He'll hang at sunrise, just as sure as there'll be a sunrise," Sheriff Harbson said. "Now go on home and get to bed. You don't want to oversleep, do you?"

There was more talk, and then the men drifted away and

things got quiet. The sheriff came back in the jail and barred the front door, and Lem heard him talking to the deputies, allowing that Lem Dyer might or might not be the things people said he was, but he sure was an odd one.

"Going to hang in the morning," the sheriff said, "and he's sitting back there in his cell smoking his pipe just like he always used to do out in his shack, of an evening. To look at him you'd think nothing had happened—or was going to happen."

Lem chuckled softly to himself. The sheriff was a good man. He'd gone out of his way to make Lem comfortable and bring him little things like tobacco and even a drink of whisky now and then. And when Lem had thanked him, he'd said, "Hell, I've got to hang you. Isn't that punishment enough?"

Lem puffed contentedly on his pipe and decided he should do something for the sheriff. But later on, after all this was over with.

He'd wanted to tell the sheriff that there wouldn't be any hanging, and he was wasting a lot of money building that scaffold and getting everything ready. But he couldn't without telling him about the pictures, and the looking and choosing, and he'd never told anyone about that. And perhaps it was just as well that he hadn't told him, because the scaffold was in the pictures.

He'd looked at so many pictures it'd given him a headache, and the scaffold was in all of them, and the people crowding around it, and Lem Dyer dangling by his neck. And then the deputy running out of the jail and shouting, stop, the governor just telephoned, Lem Dyer is granted a reprieve, and the people laughing at Lem hanging there and shouting back, cut him down and reprieve him.

It was nice of the governor, Lem thought, to take such an interest in him, and he'd gone on looking at pictures, trying to find one where the governor telephoned in time. There was one where Sheriff Harbson got sick just as he was leading Lem up to the scaffold, and he lay there on the ground looking terrible, and Lem didn't like that even if it did hold things up until the governor telephoned. And there was a picture where the Glenn Hotel caught on fire, but some people got hurt, and Lem didn't want that. He'd gone on looking, and finally he found a picture where the rope broke, or came untied, and he fell right through the trap to the ground. It took some time to get things ready again, and the deputy came out shouting stop before they got Lem back up on the scaffold. Then the sheriff led Lem back toward the jail, with all the people following along behind. Lem liked that picture, and it was the one he chose.

He knew it wouldn't get him out of jail, and he'd have to look at pictures again. But he wasn't in any hurry. Looking at pictures made him terribly tired, now that he was getting old. He didn't like to do it unless he had to.

That was why he'd gotten into trouble. If he'd looked at pictures he wouldn't have jumped into the river to pull out the little Olmstead girl, and he wouldn't have carried her over to Doc Beasley's house, thinking the doctor might be able to help her. Or he would have made it come out some other way. But he hadn't looked at pictures, and people had started talking about how maybe it was Lem who killed the little girl, and finally they'd taken him to court and had a trial.

Even then Lem hadn't looked at pictures. He hadn't done anything wrong, and he thought he didn't have anything to worry about. But the jury said he was guilty, and Judge Wilson said he was to hang by his neck until he was dead, and Ted Emmons, who'd grown up to be a lawyer and was looking after things for Lem, stopped smiling when he came to see him.

So Lem had looked at pictures again, and now he'd made his choice and everything would be all right.

He got up and fumbled in the dark for his can of tobacco. Suddenly the lights came on in the corridor, and footsteps shuffled in his direction.

"Visitors, Lem," the sheriff called. He stepped into sight, keys jangling, and unlocked the cell door.

Reverend Meyers, of the Glenn Center First Baptist Church,

sounded a deep-toned, "Good evening, Lem," gripped his hand, and then backed off into a corner and fussed with his hat. District Attorney Whaley nodded jerkily and tried to grin. He was middle-aged and getting a little fat and bald, but Lem remembered him as a tough kid stoning rats over at the town dump. Lem thought maybe he was feeling a little proud of the way he talked the jury into finding Lem guilty, but then—that was his job, and the people had elected him to do it.

Mr. Whaley's grin slipped away, leaving him tight-lipped. He cleared his throat noisily and said, "Well, Lem, being as it's the last night, we were—that is, I was—wondering if maybe you had something to get off your chest."

Lem sat down again and tilted back in his chair. He lit his pipe and puffed for a moment before he said slowly, "Why— no. I don't reckon I've got anything on my chest that's botherin' me enough to need getting off. I never went much to church except on Christmas Eve, and that because I liked to watch the kids more than for the religion. The Revern here would say I wasn't a religious man, but I don't think he'd call me bad. I reckon maybe I've shot one or two deer and caught a few fish out of season, because I needed the meat, and I've bet some on the races at the county fair, but a lot of men do that. I don't think I ever broke any other laws, and I never hurt nobody, and I think maybe I did help a lot of people."

"I don't think anyone would call you a bad man, Lem," Whaley said. "But even good men make mistakes, and we'd all feel better, and so would you, if you told us about it."

"I told you all I know, Mr. Whaley," Lem said. "I saw the little girl floatin' in the river, and I thought she was drownin'. I didn't know somebody'd choked her. I jumped in and pulled her out, and I remembered that sometimes drowned people could be brought to life but I didn't know how, so I ran to Doc Beasley's with her. I can't tell more than that."

Whaley stopped his pacing to fumble for a cigarette. The sheriff gave him one of his and held a match for him.

"It doesn't worry you, Lem?" Whaley asked. "You're going

to hang in the morning. You wouldn't want to die with that on your conscience, would you?"

"It don't worry me none," Lem said. "They don't hang innocent men, do they?"

"Why, no—"

"Then I got nothin' to worry about. I won't hang." He nodded his gray head and smiled peacefully.

Whaley stared at him for a moment. Then he turned abruptly and said over his shoulder, "Good luck, Lem."

"Why, thank you, Mr. Whaley."

The sheriff followed Whaley out and locked the cell door. "Just holler when you're ready, Reverend," he said.

As their footsteps faded away down the corridor, a wistful grin touched Reverend Meyers's gaunt face. He lowered his long form awkwardly onto Lem's cot. "They're worried some, Lem," he said. "They'd feel a lot better if you up and told them you did it. They're beginning to think maybe they're hanging an innocent man tomorrow."

"I can't tell them I did it if I didn't, Revern."

"Of course not, Lem. *I* know you didn't do it. So do quite a few other people. We've been working on it, Lem—working hard. Ted Emmons, and I, and some others. We didn't want to say anything to you because that might have made you start hoping, and we really didn't know if we could help you. We've finally had some luck, and we think we know who killed the child. Ted Emmons is trying right now to get hold of the governor, to get you a reprieve. All we need is a little more time."

Lem nodded. That explained the telephone call from the governor that would have come too late if he hadn't looked at the pictures and made a choice. But now everything would be all right. He'd get the reprieve, and then they would find the real murderer and let Lem out of jail, and he wouldn't have to look at pictures again. He felt happy about that, because looking at pictures tired him so.

"Ted was having some trouble getting through to the governor," the Reverend said, "but he'll keep trying all night, if he has to. Just put your trust in God, Lem, and everything will be all right."

"I haven't been worryin', Revern."

"Keep faith with God, Lem. Do you mind if I pray for you?"

"You go right ahead, Revern."

Reverend Meyers bowed his head and spoke softly. Lem didn't listen, but he watched him uneasily. He hadn't put any faith at all in God. He'd put all his faith in his pictures, and the looking and choosing, and it disturbed him to think that maybe God was showing him the pictures and letting him look and choose. He'd never thought of that before. The pictures were just something he'd always had, like ears to hear with, and a mouth to eat with, and eyes, and hands, and legs. But then—God gave out those things, too, or so he'd heard Reverend Meyers say, so maybe God was showing him the pictures.

The Reverend Meyers intoned a soft, "Amen," and Lem said, "I'll have to do some thinkin', Revern."

"How's that, Lem?"

"What you said—faith in God, and that. I'll have to do some thinkin'."

"I wish you would. And Lem—it might be that Ted won't reach the governor, or that the governor won't grant the reprieve. If that should happen, remember that the sheriff, and the district attorney, and the jury, have only done their duty as they saw it. Have charity in your heart for all men, Lem. Think of the Lord Jesus on the cross, saying, 'Father, forgive them, for they know not what they do.'"

"Sure, Revern. I'll remember."

"I'll be with you in the morning, Lem. And the sheriff will let you know right away if there's any good news."

The sheriff came for Reverend Meyers, and a moment later the lights were turned out. Lem sat in the darkness, smoking his pipe and thinking.

He couldn't remember when he'd first started seeing pictures and making choices. He'd never done it very often, even when he was young, because it left him dizzy and kind of sick to his stomach, and sometimes he felt so weak afterward that it scared him. But whenever he wanted something real bad he would sit down somewhere and close his eyes and think about what it was he wanted. The pictures would come, one after the other. It was like slowly flipping through a deck of cards and taking time to look carefully at each one. When he found the picture he wanted he would choose that one, and that's the way things would happen.

The other kids envied him. They said Lem Dyer was the luckiest kid in three counties. He was always getting chances to run errands and do little things for people to earn spending money, but it wasn't luck. It was because of the pictures. If he wanted a stick of candy, all he had to do was find a picture where some lady was leaving Crib's Store with an armful of groceries and looking for someone to help her. He would choose that one and run down to Crib's Store, and whoever it was would come out and give him a penny to carry her groceries. He was always there when Mr. Jones wanted the sidewalk swept in front of his barber shop, or when Banker Goldman wanted something run over to the post office in a hurry and everyone in the bank was busy. He didn't realize yet that it was his choosing that made people want things done.

He couldn't understand why the other kids didn't look at pictures when they wanted things. He was maybe nine or ten when he and some of his friends were stretched out on the river bank talking, and Stubby Smith went on and on about how much he wanted a bicycle. Lem said, "If you really want one, why don't you get it?"

The kids hooted at him and asked him why *he* didn't get one. Lem had never thought about getting something big, like a bicycle. He closed his eyes and looked at pictures until he found one where little Lydia Morrow toddled into the street in front of a runaway team, and Lem jumped after her and pulled her back, and Mr. Morrow took Lem right into his hardware store and gave him the bicycle he had in the window.

Lem chose that one. He ran up town and got to Morrow's

Hardware Store just as Lydia started into the street, and he was back at the river an hour later with his new bicycle.

For a long time Lem thought the pictures he saw were just pictures of things that were going to happen. He'd been almost grown up before he understood that his choosing a thing made it happen. Before a horse race at the county fair, he could see pictures of every horse in the race winning. If he made a choice, so he could bet on a horse, that horse would always win. He learned in a hurry that it wasn't smart to win all the time, and usually he would bet without even looking at pictures, but he always won enough money at the fair to last him through the winter.

Lem was twelve when his father fell off the barn, and he had to leave school and work the farm. He was only twenty when his mother died, and he rented out the farm and built himself a shack back in the woods, near the river, and that was his home. He loved to hunt and fish, and he loved being outdoors. As he got older a lot of people said it was a shame, a healthy man like him not working, and getting married, and raising a family. But he liked living alone, and he had all the company he ever wanted because all the kids liked to play down by the river, winter and summer. It never cost him much to live, and if he needed anything he could look at pictures and get what he wanted. If he felt like working for a week or two, he could look at pictures and then walk in to town and find a job waiting for him.

He'd had a happy life. He could choose a nice day, if he wanted to go fishing, or snow, if he wanted to do some tracking, or rain, if the farmers were having trouble about their crops. When hunting season opened, Lem Dyer always got the first and biggest buck. He never went fishing without coming back with a nice string. And if a man needed help, chances were that Lem could help him.

He'd never told anyone about the pictures, and it bothered him, now that he was sixty-one, to think that maybe it was God who was showing them to him. He wondered if God had wanted him to do something important with them—something big, like stopping wars, or getting the right man elected president, or catching criminals. He knew he could have done all those things, if he'd thought of them. There wasn't anything he couldn't do just by seeing it in a picture and choosing it.

But he never read the papers, and he'd never thought much about the world outside Glenn Center. He was almost too old to start, but he'd think some more about it, after he got out of jail. Maybe he should do something about those Russians so many people were worried about.

The clock on the Methodist Church was striking two when Lem finally went to bed.

The sheriff brought him his breakfast at four o'clock, a big plate of ham and eggs, and toast, and lots of steaming coffee. Lem could already hear the men arriving out behind the jail, where the scaffold was.

Reverend Meyers came in before Lem finished eating, and his thin face was pale and grim. "Ted is still trying," he said.

Lem nodded. He wanted to tell the Reverend that everything would be all right, so he wouldn't worry, but if he did that he might have to tell him about the pictures. The Reverend was a good man, and Lem was sure he could trust him if he trusted anybody.

He was still thinking about it when he finished his breakfast. He got down on his knees to pray when the Reverend asked him to, and then the sheriff came in and there wasn't time. The sheriff and two deputies took Lem out to the scaffold, with the Reverend following along behind them.

Lem hadn't known that he had so many friends. The crowd filled the whole field and overflowed out into First Avenue. There weren't any women and children, of course, but it looked like every man from Glenn Center and from miles around had turned out. Lem thought it was nice of them to get up so early in the morning just for him. They waited quietly, not talking much and looking the other way when Lem looked down at them.

The Reverend was talking with the sheriff at the edge of the scaffold, talking fast, and with his hands gesturing urgently. The sheriff kept shrugging and turning his hands palms up and glancing at his watch. A deputy moved Lem over the trap and put the rope around his neck. Lem looked up and smiled a little when he saw it was an old rope.

The sheriff's hands were trembling when he stepped forward. He patted Lem on the back, and the Reverend said a little prayer and whispered, "God bless you, Lem," and out in the crowd Lem saw District Attorney Whaley turn slowly and stand with his eyes on the steeple of the Methodist Church. Then there was nothing under Lem's feet, and he was falling.

The savage jerk blurred his eyes with pain, but he kept falling until he sank to his knees on the ground under the scaffold. The air rocked with noise as everyone started talking and shouting. Sheriff Harbson came down and helped Lem out and stood there white-faced, staring, not able to talk.

"Get a new rope!" someone shouted, and the crowd began to chant, "New rope! New rope!"

"You can't hang a man twice in one day," the Reverend was shouting, and the sheriff found his voice and shouted back, "He has to hang by his neck until dead. That's the law."

Then everyone turned toward the jail, where a deputy was screaming and trying to fight his way through the crowd.

The sheriff, and the deputies, and Reverend Meyers took Lem and started back to the jail with him. It took a long time, because none of the crowd seemed in any hurry to get out of their way. Lem had supposed that the men would be glad to hear about the governor's reprieve, but they weren't. The noise got louder and louder, and they were shouting foul things like he'd heard in his cell the night before. Lem's neck pained him, and his ankle hurt from the fall, and he was glad it was over with.

They'd rounded the corner of the jail and started for the entrance, on Main Street, when the roaring fury of the crowd caught up with them and overwhelmed them. The sheriff went down trying to draw his revolver and was trampled. A deputy rushed into the jail and barred the door, and he could be seen through the window excitedly bending over the telephone. The crowd boosted a man up the side of the building to jerk the wires loose. Stones shattered the window and rained into the jail.

Lem was dragged back toward the scaffold, and when a deputy ducked behind it and fired into the air, the crowd turned the other way and dragged him toward Main Street.

"Get a rope!" someone shouted.

"Anyone got a horse? They used to use horses!"

"Don't need no horse. We can use Jake Arnson's truck. Jake, back your truck under that elm tree!"

Jake Arnson ran down the street to his truck. The motor coughed and sputtered and finally caught with a roar, and the truck lurched backward. Jake parked under the elm, cut the motor, and jumped out. A rope snaked up over a tree limb. Lem had been too stunned and horrified to feel the kicks and blows that rained upon him. They hoisted him onto the truck, and he stood there, hands and feet bound, trembling with frustration, while the rope was knotted about his neck.

He told himself he should have waited to see all of the picture. He should have looked at more pictures. But how could he have known that these men he knew so well would use him like this? Now he'd have to look at pictures again. He closed his eyes and forced himself to concentrate.

The pictures flashed in front of him, one after the other, and in each of them the truck rocked forward and left Lem Dyer dangling by his neck.

Jake was back in his truck, trying to start the motor. The starter whined fretfully. Someone yelled, "Need a push, Jake?"

Lem kept watching the pictures, but finally he knew, with a sickening certainty, that pictures couldn't help him. In all of them the truck moved forward and left him hanging. It had never happened that way before—pictures without any choices.

He shook the perspiration from his eyes and looked about

him. The sheriff lay on the sidewalk in front of the jail in a pool of blood. Reverend Meyers lay nearby, his arms moving feebly, one leg bent at a strange angle. Men were hurling stones at the scaffold, where the deputy had taken refuge.

Sadly he looked down at the hate-twisted faces of men he'd thought were his friends. He remembered what the Reverend had told him. Jesus had seen hate like that when they'd nailed him to the cross, and he'd said, "Father, forgive them, for they know not what they do." Lem said the words to himself, softly. Maybe his old life wasn't worth much to anyone but himself, but it was sad.

The starter whined again, and someone called, "Speech! Can the murderer talk? Let's have a confession!"

A hundred coarse echoes sounded. "Confession! Confession!"

Lem threw his cracked voice out over the mob. "You're evil men—evil! Get down on your knees and pray that God won't punish you!"

They flung back at him wave after stinging wave of hoots and laughter. "You dirty murderer! God won't punish *us!*"

The Reverend had slumped forward to lie motionless. Doc Beasley had finally managed to push through the crowd and was kneeling beside the sheriff. The faces below Lem blurred and twisted and mortal anger overwhelmed him. "If God won't punish you," he screamed, "I will!"

He closed his eyes and willed the pictures into being. Larger than life, they were, but they moved so slowly, and he had so little time.

A tornado, dragging its swirling funnel along Main Street, relentlessly flattening buildings, crushing their occupants, toppling the Methodist Church steeple onto the jail . . .

"Not enough!" Lem gasped.

A prairie fire, tossed high on gale winds, roaring hungrily down on Glenn Center, driving the populace before it . . .

"Not enough!"

Fleets of enemy planes darkening the sky, pouring searing

death onto even such an insignificant dot on the map as Glenn Center . . .

"Not enough!"

The summer sun, high and bright at noonday, suddenly bulging crazily, tearing the sky asunder, drenching the countryside in blinding incandescence, charring human vermin, steaming away the rivers, crumbling concrete, boiling the very dust underfoot . . .

Lem chose that one, just as Jake Arnson got his motor started.

5

SECRET WEAPON

He was a tall, broad-shouldered, collegiate-looking young man wearing a neat crewcut, an outrageously patterned sport shirt, and—in spite of his obvious weariness—a ready smile. He carried a small suitcase, and he paused for a moment in the shade to survey the quiet residential street skeptically before he moved slowly up the walk to the first house.

He rang the bell and stepped back, whistling cheerfully. The door opened a crack. A woman's voice snapped, "I don't want any!" The door slammed.

He bowed solemnly at the closed door and turned away. A small boy hopped out from behind a shrub and stared at him, freckled face tense with immodest curiosity.

"Watcha sellin', mister?"

"Not selling a thing, son," he said. "I'm giving things away."

He rang the bell at the next house, got no response, and turned away sadly. The boy popped into sight again, this time from behind a hedge. "Watcha givin' away?"

"Shoelaces," he said.

The door of the third house was opened by a red-faced, bosomy blonde who regarded him with consternation. "Oh,

God!" she exclaimed. "More magazine subscriptions. We average three of you guys a week."

"Jeff Flowers is my name," he said, handing her a smartly engraved card. "I represent *New for Old, Incorporated*. Do you have any old shoelaces you'd like to dispose of?"

She scrutinized the card with a comically puzzled look on her face and suddenly doubled up with laughter. There was a faint trace of alcohol on her breath. Flowers sniffed hungrily.

"Give me that line again!" she gasped.

"Do you have any old shoelaces you'd like to dispose of?"

She giggled. "Don't tell me, now—don't tell me. Let me guess. If I buy six pairs of shoes, you'll throw in the laces free of charge?"

"No, ma'am—"

"If I buy a thousand pairs of laces, I get a pair of shoes free?"

Opening the suitcase, Flowers lifted out a tray filled to overflowing with shoelaces. There were red, orange, yellow, green, blue, purple, brown, black and white laces, of all sizes and all shades. There were plaid shoelaces and polka dot shoelaces. There were shoelaces gold-tipped and silver-tipped and plastic-tipped and jewel-studded.

"These shoelaces," Flowers said, "are finest quality and the latest style. They're guaranteed to last the life of any two pairs of shoes you want to wear them in. For any pair of old shoelaces you wish to dispose of, I'll give you your choice of any pair of new shoelaces."

She bent over the tray. "Pretty things. What do they cost?"

"They are not for sale, ma'am. They are only for trade. One new pair for one old pair."

She selected a chartreuse and brown plaid with gold tips. "These would look nice with a new summer outfit I have. How much?"

"One pair of old shoelaces."

She dropped the laces back onto the tray. "Cut the comedy. What's the price?"

"One pair of old shoelaces."

"Do you actually mean to tell me you'll take a pair of old laces—"

"Absolutely. For any old pair, you get a new pair of your choice." He grinned. "No strings attached."

"Just a minute," she said.

She was back a moment later, handing him two soiled, much-abused brown shoelaces. He knotted them together and dropped them into his suitcase.

"I get my choice?" she asked.

"You certainly do."

She picked up the plaid, gold-tipped pair. "That's all there is to it?"

"That's all."

She examined the new laces doubtfully, stretched them out, tugged at them, wadded them up. "There's got to be a catch somewhere. Is there any limit?"

"No limit at all. One pair or a thousand—a new pair for every old pair you give me."

"Come in," she said.

He sat down in the cool living room and waited. She returned five minutes later, breathing heavily. "Got every shoelace in the house," she announced, dumping them onto the sofa beside him. "Twelve pairs."

He separated them into pairs, knotted them together, and counted. "Twelve," he agreed. "Help yourself."

She did, stirring critically through the display of laces and mulling over her choices. "Twelve," she counted finally.

"I thank you very much," Flowers said.

"Look. There's *got* to be a catch somewhere."

"No catch. Let me show you." He took a glittering gadget from his suitcase. "We'll put one of the old shoelaces in here —like this, see how it clamps in? Turn the crank and see if you can break it."

She gave the crank a quick turn. The shoelace snapped.

"Now we'll try one of the new laces," he said.

He clamped it in place, and her arm bulged as she strained at the crank. Nothing happened.

"You can't break one," he said, "and you can't wear one out. We guarantee them for the life of two pairs of shoes, but actually they'll last you a lifetime."

He replaced the gadget and the tray, snapped the suitcase shut, and got to his feet. "Remember my company's name," he said. "NEW FOR OLD, INCORPORATED. You'll be hearing more about it."

"I hope you don't think you'll make a living at this."

Flowers flashed a smile. "Fortunately I don't have to take a commission in old shoelaces. I'm on salary."

The boy was waiting for him at the sidewalk. "You really givin' away shoelaces?" he demanded.

"Not exactly," Flowers said. "I'm trading them. Let's see yours. Oh—too bad. You have straps instead of laces. Sorry, but we can't do business."

He walked on to the next house, leaving the boy staring after him.

Some dozens of houses and a couple of hours later, Flowers wearily returned to his car and started in search of a restaurant. Carrying his suitcase with him, he took a seat at the counter of a small cafe, ordered coffee and a pair of hamburgers, and then turned to make a professional appraisal of any shoelaces that might be in evidence.

Three stools away from him another customer set down his coffee cup, flexed his brawny arms absently, and asked, "Think it'll ever get around to raining?"

"It'll have to get around to it sooner or later," Flowers said agreeably.

"It better. Hasn't rained for over a month, and the radio said this morning that the farmers are hit pretty bad. They're bringing in some guy that says he can make it rain. One of those deals where they drop stuff out of an airplane."

"More power to him," Flowers said. "Will they let us know when, or do we have to start carrying raincoats all the time?"

"That's a good one. Aw, it probably won't work." He glanced curiously at the suitcase. "What's your line?"

"Shoelaces," Flowers said. He opened the suitcase and set the tray of shoelaces on the counter.

The waitress paused with a cup of coffee in each hand. "Say —those are pretty."

"Aren't they?" Flowers agreed.

She served the coffee and hurried back. "What do they cost?"

"They aren't for sale. I'll arrange a trade with you, though."

"Oh, no you don't! I'll buy for cash or not at all."

"I'll trade you," Flowers said quickly, "for a pair of old shoe-laces."

The waitress turned huffily and stalked away. She was back a moment later with Flowers' order, shoving the tray of shoe-laces aside to plop the coffee and sandwiches down in front of him. She departed without speaking.

"You ought to have a better line than that," Flowers' neighbor observed.

"I suppose so," Flowers said. "Unfortunately, that's the way it has to be. The boss won't let me sell them. You trade me an old pair for a new pair, or you don't get any."

"Is that a fact? You giving me straight dope?"

"Absolutely."

"You mean you'll take these old laces I'm wearing and give me a new pair?"

"Try me and see."

The man leaned over and began yanking out his laces. "You'd better be telling the truth," he growled, "or *you're* going to put these back in."

He handed them to Flowers. Dirty black. Flowers passed the tray to him, and he selected a clean black pair in return. The waitress, watching the transaction incredulously, closed her mouth with a snap and stooped down behind the counter. She exchanged a soiled white pair for white with blue polka dots. Flowers passed out his cards.

"What do you get out of this?" the man asked.

"A pay envelope," Flowers said.

"Yeah. What does your boss get out of it?"

"A lot of used shoelaces."

"W.... ..t good are they? I mean, is this some new product ..... J introducing, or something?"

"I'll tell you how it is," Flowers said. "Have you ever noticed how you always get some polish on your laces when you shine your shoes?"

"Yeah, I guess you do if you don't take 'em out."

"My boss has developed a new process. He extracts that polish from the used shoelaces and cans it and sells it."

The man stared for perhaps thirty-five seconds before he grabbed his check and left. The waitress stalked away again. Flowers shrugged and bit into a sandwich.

A newcomer slid onto the stool beside him, reached for a menu, and said, "Think we'll ever get some rain?"

"Let's talk about shoelaces," Flowers said.

New for Old, Incorporated, had its headquarters in a tiny side-street shop in the business district. In the window was a dazzling assortment of shoelaces and a sign, *Used shoelaces wanted. Come in and trade. One new pair for each old pair you bring in.*

A bell tinkled as Flowers opened the door. He winked familiarly at the young lady who occupied a desk in one corner of the room, assured himself that there were no customers browsing among the shoelace-laden counters and tables, and gave her a robust embrace.

"You're late," she murmured. "Have a good day?"

"Don't I always?" he asked. He grimaced at the overwhelming quantity of laces that surrounded them. "After I leave this job I wear nothing but laceless shoes for the rest of my life. Did you have a good day, Miss Star?"

She smiled teasingly. "Fair."

"Dancing tonight?"

It was a rhetorical question. She smiled again and said, "The boss wants to see you."

"Fancy that. What'd I do wrong?"

"Nothing. He's going out of town for a few days, and he
wants to tell you I'm boss while he's gone."

"What a delicious thought! I've been working too hard, you
know. A really considerate boss would order me to take an
afternoon off. And since you're the boss, you can give yourself
an afternoon off. We'll go on a picnic."

"Can't you take this job seriously?"

"I cannot," Flowers said. "I know the pay is magnificent, and
I know that Mr. Vandenberg gives every indication of being
more affluent than a U.S. Mint. All the same, I can't see the
future in trading shoelaces. I want to get myself an honest
job so we can get married."

"What's wrong with getting married on this job?"

Flowers shook his head. "Eventually we're going to corner
the market with these non-breakable, last-a-lifetime shoelaces,
and where will that leave us?"

"But we'll be branching out into other things before long.
Mr. Vandenberg says—"

"I know what he says. I also know there can't be much
profit—if any—in trading new things for old. It doesn't take a
business genius to figure that out."

"I still think this is some kind of a promotion stunt."

Flowers snorted. "Whoever heard of a promotion without
publicity? The only people breathing a word about this are a
few gullible door-to-door men and you here in the shop."

He emptied his collection of used shoelaces onto her desk.
She sighed and started to count them. "Better go see Mr.
Vandenberg," she said.

Flowers went down a narrow passageway, knocked, and
opened a door at the command of a deep, nasal voice. Mr.
A. Vandenberg—if he had a first name it had remained his own
guilty secret—glanced up from a pile of newspapers. Newspapers were one of Mr. A. Vandenberg's many peculiarities.
His cramped office looked like a back-issue warehouse. Newspapers were piled in, under, and on anything that could
conceivably hold newspapers. Newspapers from all over the
world, in a multitude of languages. A casual observer would

have taken Mr. A. Vandenberg for the director of a global clipping service, rather than a used-shoelace tycoon.

Another of Vandenberg's peculiarities was his face. His leathery, oily skin hung in sagging folds on a countenance that was abnormally large and absolutely devoid of expression. In all fairness Flowers had to admit that events calling for an extreme emotional reaction were rare in the used-shoelace business. On the infrequent occasions when they did occur, Vandenberg's face registered neither displeasure nor approval, but his large, greenish eyes studied his employees with a speculative intensity that vaguely reminded Flowers of an owl staring at a mouse. Flowers did not like Mr. Vandenberg.

"Did you have a good day?" Vandenberg asked.

"Pretty good," Flowers said, absently contemplating Vandenberg's thick, unruly hair. On the first day of his employment he had pronounced that well-nourished thatch to be a wig, and he'd been speculating about it ever since. Thus far he had resisted temptation to resolve the issue with a firm, definitive tug. "A few over three hundred," he said.

Vandenberg's expression did not change. "Wonderful," his monotone rumbled. "That's a new record, isn't it? Have you drawn your replacements?"

"Janet's counting the returns now."

Vandenberg's nod seemed to originate in the general area of his protruding stomach. "I find it necessary to be out of town for a few days. Miss Star will handle the territorial assignments. I trust that no complications will arise."

"They never do," Flowers said.

Vandenberg gave him his jerky nod of dismissal; Flowers stubbornly held his ground. The green eyes scrutinized him for a moment. "Is there anything else?"

"No, sir. Except that I'd like to give notice. No particular hurry. Whenever you're able to replace me."

Vandenberg slowly settled back into his chair, his unblinking eyes fixed upon Flowers. "You don't like to work for me? Why is that? You do better than anyone else."

"Oh, I don't mind the work. It's just that I don't seem to understand this business. I can't see much future in it."

Vandenberg leaned forward stiffly. "It has a wonderful future. Especially for you. As soon as this territory is properly developed, we'll be opening branch offices. I plan to put you in charge of one of them, and eventually I'll want you to supervise branch offices in several states." He lurched to his feet. "That's in the future, of course. I'll raise your salary twenty dollars a week for the present and double it when you take charge of a brance office. Satisfactory?"

"Well—"

Vandenberg's impassive voice rumbled on while he gently patted Flowers on the back in the most approved fatherly manner. Flowers left the office a bit dazed.

"I offered my resignation," he told Janet.

"You *didn't!*" she cried.

"He turned it down and raised me twenty a week. I'm to take charge of a branch office when this territory is fully developed—whatever that means—at double what I'm getting now."

"Jeff!" she shrieked. "Then—"

"Yep. There must be something about this business that escapes me. Want to set a date?"

Mr. A. Vandenberg left his office a few minutes later. The spectacle that he encountered in the front room so disgusted and dismayed him that he retraced his steps and left by the rear door.

He drove into the country, and by dark he had reached an abandoned farm some forty miles distant. Its abandonment had occasioned talk among neighboring farmers. It was a shame, they said, to waste such good land. The new owner, Mr. A. Vandenberg, had no interest either in farming or in the opinions of his neighbors.

He drove down a weed-choked lane, left his car in a rickety shed, and strolled across a rolling, sun-parched pasture. At precisely 10:00 P.M. a looming, dark object descended. Vandenberg climbed aboard, where he was received with considerable ceremony and addressed in an unearthly tongue as General Vrooz. The dark object shot upward, moving so quickly that radar instruments at a nearby air base had only the time to acknowledge its presence with a noncommittal flicker.

As the dark object flashed outward from Earth, Mr. A. Vandenberg underwent transformation. He removed unruly hair, sagging face, bulging stomach, and everything else. *Everything.* It would have been no minor shock to Jeff Flowers had he known that the suspected wig extended to the soles of the feet. General Vrooz emerged from the pupal Vandenberg, swabbed himself off with the co-ordinated efforts of six spidery arms, preened his scaly hide carefully, and then took his place at an observation port to gaze scornfully with a trio of multi-faceted eyes at the rapidly retreating disc of the planet Earth.

He was landed in a cavern on the dark side of Earth's lone satellite. An aide took charge of the dozen pounds of clippings he had culled from the target planet's newspapers, and Vrooz worked busily on a report until the Sector Commander summoned him.

He reported to his superior in a vast, crystalline conference room. "Our approach," he announced, "is economic."

The Sector Commander waved three of his six arms in assent. "I suspected it would be, from the preliminary reports."

"We're commencing operations in one of the leading political and economic entities. The economic complex is delicately balanced—production, distribution and consumption. We intend to remove consumption from that cycle. I estimate that a twenty-five per cent disruption would collapse the entire system."

"How do you intend to proceed?"

"We shall simply trade new articles for old articles. The inhabitants will satisfy their wants by trading with us, and without consumption the production and distribution phases cannot function. Chaos will result. For example, the principal mode of transportation employs a machine called an automobile. It is the end product of a very large industry, and in its operation it utilizes a fuel called gasoline, which is the end product of another large industry. We shall offer a substitute product, trading new for old. Our substitute will be vastly superior to the native machine, and it will extract its fuel directly from the atmosphere. This will eliminate the consumption of both automobiles and gasoline, and at one stroke we shall have demolished two vital industries."

"Shrewd planning. How are the initial experiments progressing?"

"Satisfactorily. The natives possess an innate suspicion that I did not anticipate, but once that suspicion is allayed they succumb with gratifying rapidity."

The Sector Commander coldly studied a monstrous globe of the planet Earth. "We'll have to give the fleet ample notice, you know. There were complaints that we moved too quickly in the Hanolff conquest."

"That was an entirely different type of operation," General Vrooz said. "I cannot set a date, as yet, but the military will have more than sufficient notice."

"What product are you using for your experiments?"

"Shoelaces."

"*Shoe—laces?* What is that?"

"It's untranslatable. You see, the natives' footwear—"

He fumbled his explanation and finally had to have A. Vandenberg's shoes brought in.

"Shoelaces," the Sector Commander murmured. "Their technology is certainly primitive."

"Not all of their footwear requires laces," General Vrooz said, "but the majority does. It's a common article, and because it's inexpensive it enables us to exploit their greed without arousing their suspicion unduly. It is serving our purpose well."

"Excellent. But how did you happen to decide upon this?"

General Vrooz's scaly sides twitched convulsively. "If you

will pardon the levity, sir—I'm making use of a native proverb. Something about starting a new business on a shoestring."

General Vrooz returned to Earth and reluctantly re-encumbered himself with the synthetic epidermis of A. Vandenberg. Jeff Flowers and ten other male employees continued to barter shoelaces with receptive housewives. An increasing number of passers-by stopped to stare at the sign in the shop window, and so many responded that Janet Star had to install a row of chairs for the use of customers removing and replacing shoelaces.

From a slow beginning the word began to spread with awesome velocity. Startled housewives hurried to their telephones to notify sisters, cousins, aunts, neighbors and chance acquaintances. "A young man came to the door this afternoon and do you know what he *did?* You'll never believe it. He gave me eight pairs of new shoelaces for eight old pairs. And they're *beautiful!*"

The amused businessman whose curiosity led him into the New for Old, Incorporated, shop returned on Saturday with his wife and children so they could pick out their own laces. Dozens of innocent door-to-door salesmen found themselves greeted with startling enthusiasm on the chance that they might be trading something new for something old. Jeff Flowers chalked up a record seven hundred exchanges in one day. Mr. A. Vandenberg stoically tabulated the daily totals and began to pick out sites for branch offices. New for Old, Incorporated, was ready to start expanding.

The afternoon was precisely like any other afternoon of the preceding weeks, meaning that it was smoldering hot. The most that could be said was that it gave people something to talk about—the heat and the dryness.

Jeff Flowers moved wearily along a residential street. His mind was not on his work. The first of the week he was scheduled to open a branch office in Seattle, a location he'd picked himself after checking carefully to make certain that

Seattle was neither hot nor dry. Janet was staying behind until she could break in a new assistant for Mr. Vandenberg, and then she would transfer to his Seattle office. They would be married. The total of their combined salaries was almost phenomenal enough to quiet Flowers' misgivings about the future in trading something new for something old.

In the meantime, there were shoelaces to trade. Word of his coming preceded him along the street. The housewives had their doors open and neat piles of shoelaces waiting for him. If it hadn't been so infernally hot, he might have been able to run up a new record. But it was just too hot to move fast.

He mopped his brow with a handkerchief that had long since reached its saturation point and glanced at the sky. Dark clouds were drifting in over the city. He collected a total of fifteen pairs of used shoelaces at the next house, and by the time the delighted housewife had completed her selections, an occasional drop of rain was spattering against the windows.

Walking briskly, Flowers started toward his car. His walk changed to a trot and then to a headlong gallop as the heavy clouds suddenly dumped torrents of rain on the city. The long drought was over.

Half a block from his car, legs churning frantically, Flowers kicked off a shoe. He retrieved it and ran on in his sock. Another five steps and he lost the other shoe. He reached his car in a thoroughly drenched condition, suitcase in one hand and pair of shoes in the other, and flung himself into the front seat. He slammed the door, breathed a deep sigh of relief, and turned his attention to his shoes.

The reason for their irresponsible behavior smote him at one glance. He had no shoelaces.

He stared at the shoes for a long time while water drummed thunderously on the roof above him and dripped from his trousers onto the floor below him. Then, heart beating violently, he took a bright New for Old, Incorporated shoelace from his suitcase, rolled down his window, and held it out to the mercy of the downpour. Its bright color vanished. It quickly became a slimy, sticky mess and suddenly it disappeared. Even the metal tips dissolved.

Flowers repeated the experiment twice, and then he sat hunched over his steering wheel, lost in thought. Rain flooded against his windshield. He started the motor and turned on the wipers; they made scarcely a ripple in the cascading rain. Street lights were on, pallid globs of whiteness that added almost nothing to the near-zero visibility. Driving was impossible. Flowers took a deep breath and edged away from the curb.

Twenty minutes and one dented fender later, he reached a drugstore. He made a dash for it, leaving his shoes in the car. He found that he was not alone in the matter of unconventional footwear. There were at least a dozen pairs of sopped socks and stockings in the place, and their owners were talking and gesticulating furiously. Something about shoelaces.

Flowers hurried into a phone booth and dialed New for Old, Incorporated. "Janet," he said. "Now listen carefully. You've got to get out of there. Those damned shoelaces dissolve in water, and heaven knows how many thousand people were caught wearing them in this rain. There's no telling what will happen. Get over to your apartment and I'll meet you there. I think we'd better beat it out of town."

"I can't!" Janet wailed. "The police are here now and—"

"I'll take that, miss," a masculine voice snapped. "Hello. Who is this?"

Flowers banged down the phone and fled.

Back in his car, he searched in his suitcase for a pair of old laces and got his shoes securely attached to his feet. He mentally crossed his fingers and started off again.

The rain had diminished to a steady downpour by the time he reached New for Old, Incorporated. The shop was locked. He marched resolutely to police headquarters, where he found Mr. A. Vandenberg, Janet, three fellow employees, and a police sergeant who cheerfully checked off his name and invited him to join the others.

"These phony shoelaces are your responsibility," Flowers told Vandenberg. "What are you going to do about it?"

Vandenberg stood by the window staring hypnotically at the deluge. "Rain," he muttered. "Water. Rain. Water."

"Sure. And every pair of those laces is guaranteed to last the life of any two pairs of shoes."

"We shall replace every pair," Vandenberg said absently. "We shall produce a new shoelace that is not affected by this —rain."

"We'll be lucky if somebody doesn't lynch us first. There are thousands of people running around in their stockings this afternoon because of New for Old, Incorporated. I passed a shoe store on my way down here, and the place was jammed with people buying shoelaces."

"We shall replace them," Vandenberg said, leaning forward to watch rivulets of water on the window. "We shall give them two pairs for every pair of the others."

"He just doesn't understand," Janet said tearfully. "He's in a terrible lot of trouble—all of us are. It isn't because of the shoelaces, but they'll probably bring that up, too. Especially since all the policemen—"

"What about the policemen?" Flowers asked.

"A lot of them ate at that cafeteria across the street from the shop. They saw the sign in the window, and by now I suppose the entire police force is wearing our shoelaces. *Was* wearing them, I mean. Some of them came in right after it started raining and made a big fuss. And then some men came from the District Attorney's office—"

"What *is* this all about?"

"I don't know. We're all in a lot of trouble and he won't do anything about it."

"Vandenberg!" Flowers called. "How about hiring a lawyer and getting us out of here."

"Lawyer?" Vandenberg echoed blankly.

It was Flowers who finally summoned the lawyer, an austere, gloomy-looking man with a long, mournful face, horn-rimmed glasses, and enough gold in his teeth to radiate a less funereal countenance. He conferred briefly with Flowers, made a noble but unsuccessful attempt to engage Vandenberg in conversation, and went off to try his luck with the police and the D.A.'s men.

He returned shaking his head dolefully. "Shoelaces aren't the big problem. There may be a fuss about them. In fact, there already is—wait until you see the evening papers—but if your boss makes good on his offer to replace them two for one with good shoestrings, that part should be all right. I don't know how he'll work the exchange, especially as concerns the shoestrings that dissolved in the rain, but that's his worry. No, the big problem isn't shoestrings. It's records."

"What records?" Flowers asked.

"That's exactly what the District Attorney wants to know. What records. Your boss was served with a subpoena a week ago. Ordered to produce his records. He says he has no records. Can't get away with that sort of thing, you know. The fact is, there may be no problem at all—that depends on what the D.A. is looking for and whether he finds it—but your boss'll have to produce the records."

"Let's talk with him," Flowers suggested.

Vandenberg listened indifferently. Records? He had no records. None at all. What difference did that make?

"My word!" the lawyer exclaimed. "Why, it makes—" He removed his glasses and somehow managed to give the impression that he was getting a better look at Vandenberg. "My good sir, you are operating a business, New for Old, Incorporated. Do you own stock in the corporation yourself?"

"Stock?" Vandenberg said noncommittally. "There is no stock."

"But if it's a corporation, there *must* be stock! There must be stockholders. Where is your list of stockholders?"

"There are no stockholders."

The lawyer smiled weakly and tried again. "Let's see, now. You are a corporation. You are incorporated under the laws of the state of—" He paused, his thin eyebrows arched expectantly.

"I don't understand," Vandenberg said.

"But you can't be incorporated if you're not incorporated! I mean—"

"Just a name," Vandenberg said.

"It *can't* be just a name! If you want to call yourself incorporated, you must incorporate!" He replaced his glasses, and his eyesight seemed to fail noticeably. He moved closer to Vandenberg. "You have employees. Certainly you have records on them."

"Twelve employees," Vandenberg said. "No records."

The lawyer removed his glasses and absently mopped his brow with them. "Payroll records?" he suggested hopefully.

"No."

"Of course you've been making the proper withholding tax deductions from your employees' salaries and forwarding them—"

"No."

Zomrigger groped for a chair and sat down heavily. "You had each of your employees complete a Form W4. If an employee completed no such form, then you withheld his tax as if he had claimed no exemptions. You deducted the withholding tax from each employee's salary and forwarded it to—"

"No," Vandenberg said. "I deducted nothing from the salaries. Why should I take my employees' money?"

Zomrigger was breathing rapidly, his long face transfixed with horror. "Did you—did you apply on Form SS4 for an employer's identification number, and deduct social security taxes from your employees, and match them with a similar amount of your own money and—"

"No."

"Federal and state unemployment taxes?"

"No."

"Did you clear your operation with the state retail sales tax people?"

For the first time Vandenberg seemed interested. "What sort of thing is that?"

"Well, now—I couldn't say, without checking, whether or not it pertains to your operations. It depends on the retail value of your shoelaces, and since you are trading, rather than selling—but you should have cleared the operation with the retail sales tax people. They might hand you a whopping big bill if it turns out that—"

"Not selling anything," Vandenberg said. "Simple transaction—trading. Nobody's business but mine."

"What arrangements did you make about the retailer's excise tax on jewelry?"

"No arrangements. Trading shoelaces, not jewelry."

"But those shoelaces of yours. Some of them have gold and silver tips, haven't they? And artificial jewels? The government is certain to demand adjustments on the tax—I think. I haven't exactly had a case just like this one." He mopped his brow again. "Articles made of, or ornamented, mounted or fitted with precious metals or imitations thereof, have a tax that amounts to ten per cent of the sales price. Surely—"

Vandenberg shook his head slowly.

"Of course you filed your own personal income tax last April. That would be, in your case, Form 1040 with Schedule C, plus the self-employment tax, and—if your gross income exceeds six hundred dollars for each of your exemptions plus four hundred dollars—a declaration of estimated tax for the current year with payment of the first quarterly installment." He looked up hopefully.

"No income," Vandenberg said. "Just used shoelaces. The government wants me to pay a tax on used shoelaces?"

"I forgot," the lawyer said hurriedly. "You're an employee of a corporation. But then there are the corporation taxes, and —no! You aren't incorporated. You just call yourself—" He slumped forward and buried his face in his hands. "Oh, my!" he moaned. He said imploringly to Flowers, "Didn't he deduct your withholding taxes or social security?"

"Nothing," Flowers said. "I never thought anything about it. It's kind of an unusual business, you know."

"It certainly is." He turned to Vandenberg. "Did you file an income tax report last year? Or the year before that? Or the year—"

"Never," Vandenberg said.

"Oh, my!" The lawyer's glasses struck the floor with a crash. He retrieved them and ruefully examined a shattered lens. "I'd better summon a few of my colleagues," he said. "This is going to be too much for one man to handle."

By late evening it was decided that the employees of New for Old, Incorporated, were innocent of wrongdoing. They were released. Vandenberg stubbornly shrugged off the suggestions of his legal advisors, refused to answer questions, refused to post bond. He went to jail without protest, and in the morning his cell was found inexplicably empty. The F.B.I. and state and local police departments were alerted, but no trace of the fugitive was found.

Jeff Flowers found himself an honest job, at the two-dollar window of the local racetrack, and married Janet Star. The government took over the assets of New for Old, Incorporated, and found itself in possession of a roomful of used shoelaces and several thousand gross of stylish new shoelaces that were mysteriously soluble in water. It never announced the disposition of this property; the suggestion of a local newspaper, that the new laces be turned over to the armed forces for use in desert maneuvers, was ignored.

For some days after the big rain, local stores did an avalanche of business in shoelaces. For weeks people talked about the gigantic shoelace swindle and little else, and for the next several years slip-ons and shoes with zippers and straps mysteriously outsold laced shoes in that territory.

"What bugs me about this," one of Flowers' racetrack customers remarked later that summer, "is that nobody can figure out *why*. Can you?"

Flowers shook his head and fingered his newly acquired mustache. He had also allowed his crewcut to grow out. "I think," he said meditatively, "that someone was stringing us."

General Vrooz, alias A. Vandenberg, left Earth. He also left the moon and the solar system. As he told his Sector Commander, there were other worlds to conquer where his efforts would be more rewarding. Of course he is not forgetting Earth. He will be back—oh, most certainly, he will be back—and on his next trip, he won't be trading shoelaces.

But as he stated in his final report, he could see no point in investing time, materials and energy in the sabotage of an economy that carried a built-in weapon of self-destruction. In two or three flibs, the general wrote—the flib is his race's unit of temporal measurement—Earth's economy will die a natural death of strangulation from its constrictive entanglement of governmental red tape, and conquest will be a simple matter.

General Vrooz does not expect to wait long.

6

THE PERFECT PUNISHMENT

I

The Dalusian Bureau of Criminology was the only one in the galaxy that maintained its own space fleet. It operated two stubby, obsolescent cargo ships of a scant five thousand ton capacity. Both were equipped with an outmoded, inefficient triple-jet drive. At fifteen-day intervals one of them would sink ponderously into its private berth in the most remote corner of Daluse's principal space port. Three days later it would rise again, its sequence-firing jets the despair of the Noise Abatement Commission and its blunt, wobbly nose the perennial worry of the port's safety engineer, who could never be quite certain that the wobble was an optical illusion.

Everyone knew what the ships were, but even in the Golden Comet Bar, where rumors thrived and multiplied like carefully cultivated bacteria, no one had the vaguest idea where they went.

"That's real odd," Lieutenant John Mohrlock said, thoughtfully swirling the bubbling liquid in his glass. "That's damned odd. They keep a tight schedule, and they certainly can't push those old tubs far on a twenty-seven day round trip. Destination unknown, eh?"

"It ain't exactly unknown," a bearded spacer chuckled.

"*They* know where they're going. But they sure don't publicize it. Why do you ask?"

"Because tomorrow I'll be a passenger on one of them."

Heads jerked, faces turned, ascending and descending glasses halted in midair. Even the Dalusian bartender pivoted slowly, staring.

Mohrlock spoke into an abrupt, ominous silence. "What I'd really like to know is whether anyone ever comes back. You might say that I'm personally concerned."

"Why, sure. I've heard—"

"Not what you've heard," Mohrlock persisted. He directed his question along the bar. "Have any of you actually known anyone who came back?"

None of them had.

"Drink up," Mohrlock said. "It's on me—my farewell party. I don't suppose money will be of much use to me after tomorrow."

He couldn't say that he hadn't been warned. They talked about Daluse as far away as Vega. Keep your nose clean on Daluse. Stay clear of the law on Daluse. Mohrlock vividly remembered the morose complaint of a spacer whose brother had been snapped up by Dalusian Justice. "They don't try to make the punishment fit the crime. They try to make it fit the criminal. They think they're the greatest criminologists in the galaxy, and no one can argue the point because no one knows what they do about it. Just stay out of trouble on Daluse."

Executive officer of the first Terran ship ever to touch down on Daluse, with a fine career ahead of him, Lieutenant John Mohrlock had every intention of staying out of trouble, on Daluse or anywhere else.

But he had been attacked without warning, without provocation, by a drunken Centaurian named Zaque. If, on later examination, his reaction seemed unnecessarily drastic, it had been none the less essential. If he hadn't defended himself vigorously, Lieutenant John Mohrlock would have reposed on the burial slab, while the Centaurian occupied the Circle of Justice.

What followed was so bizarre, so utterly fantastic, that he found it difficult to realize that he was a crucially interested participant rather than an amused spectator.

"Ah—Lieutenant John Mohrlock—this cutting weapon—this *knife* you say you were threatened with—where was it at the precise moment that you clubbed the Centaurian Zaque with the chair?"

"On the floor, I suppose. I kicked it out of his hand."

"That is already established. Precisely *where* was it on the floor?"

The Circle of Justice provided the only rational aspect to the proceedings. It actually was a circle—a large, circular table with an opening in the center. The nine jurists were seated around the table, facing inward—facing Mohrlock. Their judicial attire made them peculiar looking even for Dalusians. The robes accentuated their long, Dalusian necks. Their long necks accentuated the disproportionate smallness of their heads, and the smallness of their heads suggested a pertinent question or two concerning their claim to the largest brains in the galaxy. They were a mysterious, chauvinistic people, and they carefully segregated foreigners into restricted zones and kept to themselves except for their administration of justice.

Mohrlock never denied his guilt. That would have been silly, not only because of the crowd of witnesses, but because of the Truth Test that opened the trial. *"Did you strike the blow that terminated a human life?"*

If he'd denied it, the Truth Detector would have blown its top. On the other hand, a confession established at the onset that he was a truthful man, for whatever that was worth on Daluse. He said, "Yes," firmly. A technician detached the wire tentacles from his body and returned the Truth Detector to its cabinet under the table.

He had not been worried, not even when the questioning took a preposterous turn. Dalusian Justice, however sinister, professed none the less to be justice, and a killing done in self-defense was justifiable homicide anywhere in the galaxy. Or so he thought.

"What we would like to know is this, Lieutenant: Why did you defend yourself so emphatically against a weapon that was securely beyond your assailant's reach?"

"I didn't know it was beyond his reach. I kicked it, but I didn't see where it went. Anyway, one jump and he'd have had it again. And I didn't know what other weapons he had in those baggy pockets."

"And you have no—regrets?"

"Regrets? I didn't intend to kill the man, and I don't look back upon it with any satisfaction. I just don't see that I could have done anything differently and stayed alive—except, perhaps, not swung the chair quite so hard. He was armed, and I wasn't. I defended myself with the only weapon available, and there wasn't time to consider that Centaurians have abnormally soft heads, which I didn't know anyway."

The end came so abruptly that Mohrlock sprang to his feet in protest. The jurists arose without any discernible signal and quietly filed out. The witnesses were gone when Mohrlock turned a stunned gaze on the witness dais. The spectators, most of them officers and crewmen from Mohrlock's ship, remained seated in uneasy silence.

Doctor Fyloid, the elderly, uniformed Dalusian who had been Mohrlock's escort since his arrest, opened a hinged panel and motioned to him. At first Mohrlock had taken him for a police officer; he learned only later that the man owned the imposing title of Doctor of Criminology.

He beamed at Mohrlock. "You may leave, now."

"Then—I'm free? They've released me?"

"Of course not. You are assigned to the Department of Criminology. You will kindly present yourself at Port Entrance X-7 at 0800 tomorrow morning. You have until then to put your affairs in order."

"What kind of idiocy—"

"On Daluse," the doctor said severely, "criminology is an

exact science. We take great pains to keep it so. You will kindly remember that. Idiocy, indeed!"

Mohrlock took a deep breath. "All right. I'll be there."

"Promptness will be appreciated. Your ship lifts at precisely 0830."

Escape was out of the question. No ships were scheduled to leave Daluse, no Dalusian would have wanted to help him, and no foreigner would have dared.

His captain promised to refer the matter to a friendly embassy and explore every means of obtaining his release. Mohrlock had no personal affairs to put in order, so he gave himself one last, resounding binge and reported as ordered, seven minutes late and with a violent hangover.

Doctor Fyloid escorted him to a tiny stateroom on the ridiculous cargo ship and made a flowery little speech, attesting to his own good will and good wishes, as well as those of the Bureau of Criminology and all of the Dalusian people. Mohrlock restrained himself from slugging him, with difficulty. The doctor departed, and ten minutes later the ship was in space.

Mohrlock did not become frightened—really frightened—until he learned that he was the only passenger.

II

Hell was their destination. By some oversight it had got onto the star charts as Bal.

"It used to be Baluse," said the young cabin boy, the only member of the crew Mohrlock saw during the entire trip. "People kept getting it mixed up with Daluse, so they shortened it."

They were headed directly toward the Dalusian sun, and as the heat steadily increased in intensity the old ship's cooling apparatus proved unequal to its task. It worked in spurts, and between the spurts the temperature shot up alarmingly. "We'll be cinders before we get there," Mohrlock complained.

The cabin boy grinned. "Naw. It gets as bad as it can, and then it can't get any worse."

"Do you bring many passengers back from Bal?"

The cabin boy looked away. "Not many."

"Have you *ever* brought any back?"

"Not since I been on this run."

"What sort of place is it?"

"I dunno. The base is all underground. I ain't seen much of it."

His tone implied that he hadn't wanted to see much of it.

Mohrlock let the cabin boy return to his card game and waited pantingly for the next respite from the heat, which quickly got as bad as it could and stayed that way. On the twelfth day they moved into Bal's shadow cone, the ship's overheated plates crackling with the cold of space, and landed on the night side of as barren a world as Mohrlock had ever seen.

There was no atmosphere. A refugee from this penal colony would be quickly frozen stiff or—if the planet's period of revolution produced day and night—cooked. The Dalusians might have difficulty in keeping their prisoners alive, but they certainly wouldn't be troubled with their running away.

A black-uniformed Dalusian with an unusually prominent nose came aboard, indifferently introduced himself as Doctor Rudieb, the Base Administrator, and led Mohrlock through a frost-lined blimp tube to a multiple air lock. The cargo lock was already open, and a tractor with a bored-looking Dalusian at the controls was awaiting the signal to nudge the cargo conveyor into position.

They stomped the frost from their boots and turned into an unending, brightly lighted tunnel. Doctor Rudieb opened a door for Mohrlock. "Welcome to Bal," he said absently.

"Delighted to be here," Mohrlock drawled.

The sarcasm was lost on Doctor Rudieb. He muttered something that sounded like, "Delighted to have you," and motioned Mohrlock into a room obviously designed for the interrogation of prisoners.

Mohrlock sat down and looked about him resentfully. Psychological apparatus ringed his chair. A misplaced tentacle of a Truth Detector protruded from a cabinet. Rudieb's desk was on a higher level, and as he slit open an envelope and began shuffling papers he dropped occasional disapproving glances onto Mohrlock.

"Rather a clear-cut case," he announced finally. He sounded as though he'd hoped for something more complicated. "No tests called for."

"Are you congratulating me?" Mohrlock asked.

Rudieb screwed his features into what he probably thought was an intimidating scowl. He looked ridiculous. "We have only a few regulations, but those are enforced unconditionally. No irregularities of any kind are tolerated. Do you understand?"

Mohrlock nodded resignedly.

"I'm assigning you to Level Three. Your first regulation is that you will not leave that level unless I request or authorize that you do so. Your second regulation concerns your clothing. You will be furnished with one complete outfit of black work clothes. You may buy as much additional clothing as you like, of any style that appeals to you, but it must be black. You are forbidden to wear any apparel, even undergarments, that is not black. Do you understand?"

Mohrlock nodded.

"Your third regulation concerns money. We employ a five-week, thirty-day month, and you will receive an allowance of three hundred monetary units per month, paid weekly. This will be adequate for your normal needs and will even permit some extravagance. If you need or want more money, you may work for it. You'll find an employment agency in the Administration Building on your level. If you have more money than you need, you would be wise to bank the surplus. The bank pays a generous rate of interest on savings. You may borrow from the bank if you overspend or gamble away your allowance, but the amount you borrow, plus interest, is automatically deducted from your next week's allowance. We do not interfere with your financial affairs as long as you handle them competently.

"Your fourth regulation concerns your fellow citizens. You will find two types of citizens on your level. For convenient reference we designate them Type A and Type B. You are Type B, as are all citizens dressed in black. You are absolutely prohibited from committing any kind of crime, either felony or misdemeanor, against a Type B citizen. Crimes against Type A citizens are permitted, provided that you report them in the prescribed manner.

"Your fifth regulation concerns your quota. You will receive complete information in the mail tomorrow, along with your report forms. I ask as a personal favor that you commit no crimes until you receive the report forms. It would create unnecessary complications for my office. Have you any questions?"

Mohrlock gazed at him dazedly. "I don't understand any of it!"

Scowling irritably, Doctor Rudieb paused for a moment to massage his nose. "It isn't the least complicated. In this envelope you will find a list of the regulations, your identity card, and your allowance. This being the last day of the second week of the fourth month, I am issuing a prorated ten units for this week and your sixty units for next week. Study the regulations, and if you need further information I'm sure you will find your fellow Type B citizens helpful. And, of course, you are always free to write to me requesting an interview." He got to his feet and touched a button on his desk. "Good luck, Lieutenant John Mohrlock. I wish you a happy stay at Bal Base. A new arrival, Mr. Jones. Issue his clothing and take him to Level Three."

A black-suited Non-Dalusian had appeared quietly in the doorway. He touched a finger to his cap, beckoned to Mohrlock, and led him away.

Their first stop was a supply room. "Take your duds off," Jones said, "and we'll see if we can find something that fits you."

"Are you a prisoner, too?" Mohrlock asked, eying him curiously.

"They don't like us to say 'prisoner.' I'm a Type B citizen. But sure. Know the Golden Comet Bar in Space City?"

"I was there the night before I left."

"I held up the place. Got the day's receipts—nearly ten thousand Gold Dalusian Units. Best haul I ever made. Nearly got away with it, too. Here—put your stuff in this box. You can keep your wallet—didn't Old Blue Nose give you your allowance? But leave your outside money here. It won't buy you a bread crumb on Bal."

Mohrlock bundled his discarded clothing into the box and dressed himself in black. Jones stamped Mohrlock's identification on the box. "All set? Then I'll take you to Level Three."

"What kind of place is it?" Mohrlock asked.

"Not bad. Not bad at all."

"It sounds like an odd kind of prison."

"I think these Dalusians are nuts. I pull a big job, and all they do—come along. I gotta get back before Old Blue Nose thinks he needs me again."

They entered an enormous, sloping tunnel and rode a moving ramp interminably downward. The ascending ramp was on the opposite side, and a wide road ran between them.

Jones chatted cheerfully. "Nothing to it, really. It's almost like living anywhere. A nice town on every level, good restaurants and bars, stores that sell almost anything you'd want. The only important things is not to commit no crimes against Type B citizens and not to miss your quota. If you slip up on either of them, you're in trouble."

"What sort of quota?" Mohrlock asked.

"It depends. What are you in for?"

"I killed a man in self-defense."

"In that case, I don't know. I suppose they called it murder, or you wouldn't be here. So that'll be your quota. One or two a week, probably."

"One or two what?"

"Murders."

III

The Main Street could have been transported intact from a small town of any of a dozen worlds Mohrlock remembered. The business buildings were neat, practical structures, some of mortared stone, some faced with grooved sheets of compressed stone. The sidewalks thronged with pedestrians, men and women, Types A and B. Colorful native Dalusian costumes mingled with the somber, unvarying shade of black. There were several small ground cars parked at the curb, and occasionally one moved slowly along the street, piloted by a black-suited Type B citizen. Such an elaborate underground establishment required an enormous cavern; its distant ceiling was completely hidden by the glare of artificial sunlight.

Bewildered, fascinated, Mohrlock walked slowly to the end of the business section, circled a block, circled another block, finally backed into a chair at a little sidewalk cafe and managed to order a glass of beer from a pretty young Type A citizen waitress. While he sipped beer he watched the passers-by, and so dazed was he that the beer was gone by the time his mind had recorded a single interesting fact: Nearly all of the Type A citizens were Dalusians; nearly all of the Type B citizens were aliens.

His immediate concern was for a place to stay. He crossed the street to a tall building that bore the sign, THIRD LEVEL HOTEL. The Dalusian room clerk raised both hands in dismay when he asked for a room.

"I'm terribly sorry, sir. We have none available. I believe all three hotels are absolutely full up. I'd suggest you try a rooming house."

"Where am I likely to find one?" Mohrlock asked.

"Almost all of the private dwellings accept roomers."

Mohrlock thanked him and left with an envious glance at the luxuriously fitted lobby. He strolled along Main Street, and as soon as he reached the residential section there were shade trees, neat stone fences, and variously sized houses of a startling architectural variety. The houses had lawns of lush grass trimmed with flower beds, and he could catch an occasional glimpse of a vegetable garden in the rear.

He searched anxiously for a sign that would indicate a vacant room, but he saw none. The houses thinned out as he approached the edge of town and were widely separated by parklike lawns or gardens. He walked as far as the last cross street and then turned back disgustedly.

"Looking for someone?" asked a Type B citizen who had come up behind him. He was a small, wiry man with thick, glistening black hair.

"A rooming house," Mohrlock said.

"They're all rooming houses."

"I was looking for a sign."

"New, aren't you?" He offered his hand. "Call me Whitie."

Mohrlock shook hands with him. "John Mohrlock."

"Forget it. One name is all you need here, and you'd be wise to pick your own and sing it out loud and clear when asked. Otherwise someone'll give you one, and you might not like it. Good looking fellow like you, you'll end up being called 'Ugly.' Like I'm 'Whitie' because I have black hair. John Mohrlock—better call yourself 'Morrie.' We got too many Johnnies already. About the rooming houses. All of these places have vacancies. Most of the B's like to live uptown, so it's harder to find a room there. The hotels have waiting lists. Rooms out here cost less, and me—I like the quiet suburbs better anyway. It's up to you. Try to get settled before dark, though. The nights here are really black."

Mohrlock looked doubtfully at the intense light overhead, and Whitie chuckled. "They turn it down in the evening and off at night. We get regular days and nights, and beautiful sunsets and sunrises. If you think you'd like it out here, my landlady has plenty of rooms."

"Sounds all right to me."

Whitie's landlady, a Mrs. Lynez, was a Type A—a plump, middle-aged, colorfully dressed Dalusian. She greeted Mohrlock with polite indifference, and minutes later he found himself in possession of a spacious front room, clean, adequately furnished, and modestly priced. The ten units a week included breakfast. Upstairs rooms were available at a savings of a unit a week, but the house was not mechanized, and Mohrlock disliked the inconvenience of climbing stairs.

Whitie shook hands again and wished him good night. "I turn in early," he said, "because I get up early. I got a job at the bakery. Tomorrow's the first of the week, too, and I try to get my quota out of the way in a hurry. Be seeing you."

Mohrlock was left gazing out of his front window. Beyond the edge of town was a ripening grainfield, the tall, slender stalks rigid in the motionless air. On the distant crest of a low hill he could see farm buildings. The overhead glare had dimmed perceptibly, and the first red streaks of a synthetic sunset were visible. He shook his head in disbelief.

He went to bed early himself, without supper, and slept soundly for the first time since he'd left Daluse, and when he awoke in the morning he lay long abed in blissful relaxation. The bed was comfortable, and the room's ventilation a crisp, fresh smelling contrast to the sterile blasts of compounded air he had experienced in space. The location, except for an occasional gentle snore from Whitie's room across the hall, was deliciously quiet.

Mrs. Lynez had an enormous breakfast waiting for him when he got up—a steaming hot drink, chilled juices, a meat pie, cakes and syrup. He enjoyed the food, but her flat, unemotional voice quickly got on his nerves. She spoke complainingly and unbelievably about the weather. Her flowers and garden were badly in need of rain. He maintained a sympathetic attitude while doubting her sanity.

He left the house after breakfast, and at the Main Street intersection he turned left and strolled out into the country. What he had assumed to be a synthetic horizon kept receding before him until he had to stop in amazement to contemplate the unbelievable dimensions of this cavity—this one of several cavities—in the inhospitable rock of a half-frozen and half-baked planet. At least two miles wide, he thought it was, and a number of miles long, and—but the glare of artificial sunlight made it impossible to estimate the height of the roof's apex.

The main road ran unswervingly down the center of the cavity, with side roads crossing it at regular intervals. The land was pleasantly undulating, the crops looked well tended, and healthy meat animals grazed placidly in stone-fenced pastures. Lonely farm buildings dotted the landscape.

Midday came before he finally reached the end. The road terminated at a high stone wall that crossed the cavity from one side to the other. He sat down with his back against it and attempted to puzzle some meaning out of what he had seen.

These enormous caverns had once been mines, he thought —perhaps still were mines at their distant terminations. All highly civilized worlds replenished their exhausted mineral wealth by exploiting the uninhabited planets of their systems, and it was not unheard of for them to exile their criminals to slavery in the mines. As the Dalusian mines were automated and Dalusian criminology became more enlightened, the strange society of Type A and Type B citizens could evolve. The mines no longer needed slaves, but Dalusian society had continued to demand punishment for its criminals, albeit a more humane, scientific punishment. A perfect punishment.

That much seemed clear enough, but he was unable to carry his reasoning through to any kind of satisfactory conclusion. What *was* the punishment? A quota—a quota of crime? Could a criminal be punished by forcing him to commit additional crimes? He thought long about it, and the longer he thought, the more he became convinced that he was the victim of a bizarre joke.

Mohrlock returned to town under the riotous contortions of a synthetic sunset. As he entered the house Whitie bounded out of his room to meet him.

"I been wondering about you," he said. "Nobody saw you uptown today."

"No one knows me," Mohrlock said. "But I wasn't uptown. I went for a walk in the country."

"Without food? You shouldda got a box from Ida. She's a B—has her own business uptown, box lunches, and she does real well. Owns a house and groundcar and has a nice bank account. B's that have jobs, or get tired of the restaurants, buy her lunches. About no one knowing you, you'd be surprised. A new B isn't hard to pick out. You missed something, not being uptown today. It's the first of the week, and a lot of the B's try to get their quotas out of the way early. It's almost worth the price of admission to watch the pickpockets operating. I doubt if an A can stick his nose out on the first of the week without getting his pocket picked. Mrs. Lynez left your mail in your room. Your quota stuff, probably."

Whitie followed him into his room and watched while he ripped open the fat envelope and spilled out its contents. There was a package of large envelopes, addressed with a single word—OFFICIAL, a book of detachable forms coded for machine filing, and a quota assignment card.

LIEUTENANT JOHN MOHRLOCK
WEEKLY QUOTA: ONE MURDER

And below, in fine print: *Regulation Four: Crimes against Type B citizens are prohibited.*

Whitie slumped onto the bed and stared up at him incredulously. *"Murder?"*

"I killed a man in self-defense," Mohrlock said bitterly. "The Dalusians called it murder."

"I'm sorry, " Whitie said, avoiding his eyes. "I shouldn't have looked."

"Why should my quota be a secret?"

"It just is. A man's quota is his own business unless he wants to talk about it himself. If I was you I wouldn't mention it to anyone. We've never had a murderer on this level—not that I ever knew about. I thought maybe I could help you get started, but murder—you'll have to handle that by yourself. Are you sure you're on the right level? I had it figured that the different levels were for different kinds of crimes. We're mostly pickpockets and various kinds of robbery on Level Three. Five is supposed to be the violent level. I thought all the murderers went to Level Five."

"Doctor Rudieb said Level Three."

"Then you're in the right place. Maybe Five got crowded. Or maybe they're changing this level. I hope not. It's always been a pretty nice place."

"It doesn't make sense," Mohrlock muttered. "None of it makes sense."

"It makes a lot of sense. The way I have it figured, the Dalusians send their own criminals here as A's, and the foreign criminals as B's. Our punishment is that we have to keep on committing crimes, and their punishment is that they have to be the victims."

"Very considerate of them to let us have the better deal," Mohrlock said dryly.

"It may seem that way at first, but after a while you get to wondering. The A's don't talk much about their problems, or about anything else, but I get the idea they're just plodding along like we are, trying to save up for something and not knowing what minute some B will use them to fill a quota and there go their profits for the week. It must be hell for them, but it's no fun trying to decide who to rob next, either. I've got so I watch a man until he takes his receipts to the bank. Then I know I won't be hurting him so much."

"I say it doesn't make sense. We can rob whenever we feel like it, and yet they give us a weekly allowance?"

"That's part of the punishment—crime without profit. We have to turn in our take when we file the report. Once when I was a bit short I held out ten units, and they deducted it from my next week's allowance. With interest."

"Supposing I don't do my quota. What happens then?"

"Get that idea out of your head right now!"

"What could they do?"

"Plenty. Oh, they might dilly dally a little, impose a penalty, give you warnings—or they might not. You'd disappear, and only Old Blue Nose would know where. There are rumors—but never mind. Just do your quota and behave yourself."

"What are the rumors?"

"That you'd be sent to a lower level—"

"What would be so terrible about that?"

"As an A. If you think *committing* crimes is tough, just consider how you'd enjoy being on the receiving end."

Mohrlock examined the report forms. His name and identification were printed on the front of each card. Blanks were provided for filling in the type of crime and the location. At the bottom was a warning: *Caution: All property and money taken from the victim must be returned with this report. Crimes against Type B citizens are prohibited.*

On the reverse side was a single question: *Why did you select this victim?*

"Look," Whitie said urgently. "Lay off Mrs. Lynez, *please.* I been with her ever since I came here. She's quiet and don't say much, but she's always been nice to me. And Porky, that's the A that runs the Third L Bar. You can tell to look at him that he's worrying his heart out about something, but he never mentions it. I guess all the A's got plenty to worry about. There's old Scrubby, too, that runs the hand laundry and does a lot better job than that dratted Autolaund across the street but doesn't get much business because it takes him longer. I held him up once, when I first came here, and his whole day's receipts were only—but skip it. You'll do what you gotta do. It's just—well—we get to know some of these A's pretty well."

"Whatever I do," Mohrlock said, "I'm certainly in no hurry to be doing it."

"No. You don't have to rush it. You've got five more days."

IV

The next morning Mohrlock explored the town, from the bakery at one side to the group of small factories at the other. Everywhere it bustled with activity. There were postmen briskly making their rounds—B's, all of them, Doctor Rudieb taking no chance on someone including the mails in his robbery quota. Mohrlock smiled at the recollection of Rudieb's own black uniform. There were small trucks bringing in produce from the farms, and large trucks bringing in supplies from other levels and taking away the Third Level's surpluses.

When the stores opened Mohrlock joined the morning shoppers. He built his wardrobe up to respectable proportions, patronized a barber shop and a tobacconist, browsed absently through stores, spent some time in a ground-car showroom, and even allowed himself to be interested in displays of building materials and agricultural implements.

He turned away uneasily whenever a Type A citizen approached him. *Weekly Quota: One Murder.* They couldn't possibly expect him to take them seriously.

At a real estate office he studied listings of farm properties for sale, of town lots available for building, of vacant stores and offices where an ambitious B with money saved might develop his own business. He visited the Administration Building, which housed the bank and the post office—both staffed with B's—and opened a bank account.

In the small room marked ADMINISTRATION Mohrlock found a Type B clerk reading a book. "There seems to be some mistake about my quota," he said. "Who do I see about it?"

"Write to Doctor Rudieb," the clerk said promptly. "Was it about a revision?"

"Revision? I'm new here, and—"

"Did you receive a quota card?"

Mohrlock nodded and handed it to him. He glanced at it, glanced again, stared at Mohrlock and then at the card. "What's the mistake? Have they got you down for the wrong crime?"

"No. I mean—surely they don't expect—"

"I get you." He returned the card. "That's exactly what they expect—one murder a week."

"Would it do any good for me to write to Doctor Rudieb?"

The clerk shook his head. "If it was murder that put you in

here, murder is what you're going to do. One a week, like your card says."

"What happens if I don't?" Mohrlock asked quietly.

The clerk regarded him with interest. "In all the time I've been here, and I'd make that about eleven years, now, I've never known anyone who had the nerve to skip his quota and find out. You don't look nervy enough to be the first. You'll do your one murder a week and like it. And if you're worried about the A's, forget it. There isn't a one of them who wouldn't be better off dead."

At the sidewalk cafe Mohrlock drank beer after beer and scrutinized each A who passed. In two hours he saw only two who were not Dalusians. B's who had failed to meet their quotas? And what could the A's have done to deserve this? Were they political prisoners?

Weekly Quota: One Murder.

"I won't do it," Mohrlock announced aloud and then quickly looked up at the A waitress who was clearing the next table. She did not seem to have heard him.

At once he felt immeasurably better. He'd made his decision; he wouldn't do it. He spent the remainder of the afternoon drinking beer and enjoying the artificial sunshine.

He finished his evening meal just as the stores were closing. There was a mass exodus of the A's who worked in them, and he found himself walking behind one as he returned to his rooming house. It was an elderly little Dalusian whose wife was undoubtedly someone's landlady. Mohrlock overtook him just as he turned a corner, and they collided. Mohrlock muttered, "Sorry," and the Dalusian said softly, "I beg your pardon."

He plodded off along the side street, and Mohrlock stood watching him until he reached his house. His wife was at the door waiting for him.

Whitie was at the door waiting for Mohrlock. He said anxiously, "Did you—"

Mohrlock shook his head. "I wasn't in the mood for murder today."

"When you get around to it, better do it where there's some light. Or if you think you got to do it in the dark, be sure and ask if it's an A."

"*Ask?*" Mohrlock repeated blankly. "You mean—they'd tell?"

"Sure. A's never resist. Those of us who do armed robberies, we're issued weapons but no ammunition. We say, 'Hand over your money,' they hand over their money. If it's light you couldn't get a B by mistake, on account of the clothes. In the dark you could. If you was to try to hold up a B in the dark he'd let you know, and that would be that. But your quota being murder, if you mistook a B for an A he might not have a chance to let you know, and you'd be in big trouble. So I say—if you aren't *sure* it's an A, better ask. Just a suggestion, you being new here."

"Thanks," Mohrlock said.

Whitie was engaged. His fiancee, a gaunt, middle-aged woman whose features suggested a weird melange of planetary origins, worked in the bakery with him. They were saving their money to build a house, and Whitie had made down payments on three lots in a choice location.

Mohrlock happened onto them in a tiny restaurant that called itself the Denebian Tea Room and pretended to have an atmosphere, and they interrupted their argument long enough to invite Mohrlock to join them. "Aw, stop complaining, Bella," Whitie said. "Get it over with. It don't take long. Right, Morrie?"

"What doesn't take long?" Mohrlock asked.

"Bella always leaves her quota for the end of the week," Whitie explained. "I keep telling her—look! There's an A with her arms full of packages. Nab her before she gets away."

"Oh, all *right!*"

Bella flounced away, caught up with the woman, and rifled her dangling handbag with a motion so deft that it left Mohrlock blinking. She hurried back and sat down, breathing heavily, to fill out a report form. "'Why did you select this victim?' Bah! If I could get my hands on Old Blue Nose I'd show him a new use for fingernails. 'Because she happened to be there,' that's why." She dumped the report form and the contents of the woman's purse into an official envelope, sealed it, and tossed it to Whitie.

"Three to go," Whitie said. "Doesn't the waitress have anything in her apron pocket?"

"Just a handkerchief. I'd be ashamed to report *that*, so I put it back."

"Finish your sandwich, then, and we'll try the grocery stores. And next week, how about doing a little work on the first?"

"Bah! You can't make a dip on the first without finding two other B's already got their hands in the bag."

Whitie grinned. "How's business with you, Morrie?"

"Nothing new," Mohrlock said.

"Better get with it. Four more days, counting today."

"You mean he ain't done his quota, either?" Bella demanded.

"He's new here. Come on, swallow your sandwich."

They hurried away. Mohrlock turned in the opposite direction and walked slowly, looking into store windows.

Suddenly he saw a familiar face looking out at him. It was the Dalusian he'd collided with the night before, a nondescript clerk in a nondescript shop that sold trinkets and seemed to do very little business. Mohrlock went in and bought an ashtray for his room, though he had three already. He was waited on politely without any sign of recognition.

He could not say, afterward, what impelled him to be waiting for the clerk when he left for home that evening. Mohrlock followed discretely until the clerk turned off Main Street and then forced himself to hurry on without a backward glance.

That night he had his first nightmare. His hands were clutching the little clerk's long, Dalusian neck, and he squeezed with all of his strength, choking, choking, choking, while the arms threshed helplessly and the legs churned and a rattling, sticky death set the face in a grimace of terror. He awoke soaking with perspiration and found Whitie bending over him anxiously.

"I thought maybe somebody mistook *you* for an A," Whitie said.

"I guess I had a nightmare," Mohrlock said. "Sorry."

He lay awake until morning because he was afraid to let himself go back to sleep.

Weekly Quota: One Murder. Mohrlock attempted to thrust the word *quota* from his consciousness, but it returned. Inevitably it returned. He would overhear B's conversing— "Done your quota yet?"—or his book of report forms would catch his eye, or the word would slip into his mind of its own sinister persistence.

He had three more days in which to commit a murder. He was ordered—commanded—to murder, with horrendous consequences implied if he did not. Perhaps it *was* a just, a perfect punishment, or would have been if he were a murderer. But to force him to take a human life intentionally because he had taken one accidentally seemed a monstrous miscarriage of justice.

And to take another life next week and another the week after that, to live out his existence in this lazy, purposeless environment, murdering, murdering—

He would not do it. He'd already decided that, the issue was closed—so why did the word *quota* upset him? Why had he followed the little clerk home? Had his subconscious mind already selected his first victim?

The next night he followed the clerk home again, followed him almost to his doorstep, and stood in the dusk looking at the door long after it had closed silently behind him.

V

"It finally rained last night," Mrs. Lynez said at breakfast, her voice as devoid of feeling as it had been when she complained about the lack of rain.

"Glad to hear it," Mohrlock said good naturedly, wondering if she were joking or if her mind had taken its final plunge. But when he got outside he found the walks moist and droplets of water on the grass. That afternoon he asked Whitie about it.

"They have a sprinkling system," Whitie explained. "It doesn't exactly make rain, just a heavy mist. They only turn it on at night. It clears the air and settles the dust."

"I was wondering where the water comes from. Those two junky cargo ships certainly don't bring it in."

"The base probably reuses its water, just like a space ship. There's supposed to be a big reservoir on the lowest level, and anyway, a lot of big ships come to pick up ore. Maybe they bring water. They might as well bring something."

Mohrlock acknowledged the truth of this and revised his thinking about the cost of Dalusian criminology. The ore ships would otherwise be cruising empty on their low-cost sunward run, so supplies put down on Bal could be considered as virtually free of transportation expense. The base produced some if not most of its own food, there was an abundance of solar power on the other side of the planet, and prisoners supplied whatever labor was needed. Perhaps the small factories even manufactured things for export, and Dalusian criminology showed a modest profit.

Weekly Quota: One Murder.

Mohrlock was determined not to approach the little clerk again, so he bought one of Ida's box lunches for his evening meal and walked into the country. He spent the afternoon seated under a stunted tree watching an A farmer and his wife weed their vegetable garden. The B's had machinery; the A's were unable to save enough money for more than simple hand tools. All of their profits were snatched up by the relentless quotas of thieves and robbers and pickpockets. Mohrlock fell to pondering the meaning of life as lived by an A, wondering if he could convince himself that the murder of one of them might be considered an act of mercy.

He could not. The A's were free to take their own lives, and yet Whitie said that he'd never heard of an A suicide. Possibly their terms in the purgatory of Bal Base were limited, and their fortitude derived from the knowledge that ultimately they would be released.

The farm woman returned to the house when darkness began to fall; her husband worked on alone until it was too dark for him to see, as though defying Mohrlock to do something about it. Finally he turned toward the house, and Mohrlock wearily walked back to town.

Whitie met him with a question. "Did you—"

Mohrlock shook his head.

"Look, fellow. Tomorrow's the end of the week."

"What the hell do I care?" Mohrlock snapped.

"Sorry. Just thought I'd remind you."

Breakfast. Mrs. Lynez's flat voice. She used different words, but she seemed always to be saying the same thing. Mohrlock was out the door before her final remark registered: "This is the last day of the week."

Overheard on a street corner: "Got your quota in?"

A pickpocket joggled Mohrlock's elbow as he slapped a wallet onto the bar and began filling out a report. "That does it for this week—finally!"

Already he could sense the deadly monotony of this place. Even when different things happened, they happened in the same way. They *felt* the same, just as the humidity felt the same day after day, and the temperature felt the same, and his breakfast looked and tasted the same, and the same A's and B's could be seen every day at the same time and place dressed in the same way and doing the same things.

The little Dalusian clerk stood in the shopwindow as usual, gazing blankly at the passers-by. Mohrlock wondered if it was the man's long Dalusian neck that attracted him. His fingers seemed irresistibly drawn to it. His one ultimate purpose in life seemed to be the throttling of that Dalusian neck. He turned, passed the window again, passed it a third time. The clerk continued to gaze blankly.

At the next corner he encountered Whitie and his fiancee. They were in the final throes of their week-long argument and did not notice him. "What do you want to do—wait until they've all gone home? You only need one more. Get that one."

"Oh, all *right!*"

Mohrlock hastily turned away, thus avoiding Whitie's inevitable, "Did you—" He ducked into a bar, and two B's bought drinks for him before he could order. "Celebrating," one of them said. "Just finished our quotas. Every week we tell ourselves we'll get them out of the way early, but we never do."

Mohrlock did not thank them.

"Look at those idiots," said an elderly B who shared Mohrlock's table at the sidewalk cafe. "Half of 'em try to do their quotas on the first day of the week, and the other half wait until the last day. Me, I always work the middle. Sometimes I'm the only one operating."

Mohrlock started to walk around the block, saw a B lurking near the rear entrance of a store to waylay the proprietor, and frantically retreated into the nearest bar. "Got your quota in?" grinned the B standing next to him. Mohrlock wanted to scream at him, "No, I'm one murder short!"

He wandered into a hotel lobby and killed some time watching a fast game of *Free Fall*. The stakes were high, the players recklessly squandering what they had left of their week's allowances.

"Deal me out," said one, raking in a fat pot. "I haven't finished my quota."

"Oh, for God's sake—a quota hopper! Who let him into the game?"

Mohrlock followed him out and again walked past the little Dalusian's shop, carefully looking the other way. "If I must—" he said.

He walked past again, this time staring at the alluring neck. "If I must—" The thought gagged him, but all of his resistance had vanished, and his noble resolutions were ashes to be ground between his clenched teeth. "If I must—I must."

The clock on the Administration Building bonged the hour of closing. As soon as the stores emptied, Mohrlock walked unsteadily to the corner and took cover in the doorway of a shoe store. Lights remained on in all of the stores, the clerks rearranging stock and taking end-of-the-week inventory. Mohrlock thrust his trembling hands into his pockets and waited.

The lights began to go out, and finally the little Dalusian appeared. He walked slowly, head bowed in weariness, or deep thought, or—prayer? Mohrlock swore savagely and lurched after him, pulse pounding, breath coming in laborious, whistling gasps. He quickly caught up and followed closely behind him, and though it was nearly dark, the long, white neck gleamed palely in the dimming light and beckoned him on.

At the Dalusian's corner Mohrlock stepped forward boldly and jostled him. "Excuse me," he muttered, his hands poised to ʌeap at the enticing throat. "Can you tell me what time it is?"

"What time it is?" the Dalusian repeated. Something in his manner made Mohrlock hesitate. Clothing rustled as he reached into a pocket. "What time it is?" he said again. He searched another pocket. "I'm sorry. My watch has been stolen."

He moved off into the darkness, leaving Mohrlock staring after him numbly. The pathetic creature had been robbed and stalked by a murderer, and yet he was miraculously returning home safely.

Mohrlock wheeled and retraced his steps, intent on getting to the nearest bar. A voice snarled out of the darkness, "Stick 'em up!"

"Go to hell!" Mohrlock snapped.

The voice chuckled. "Sorry. Couldn't see you was a B. Seen any A's around here?"

"No."

"Drat it! Guess I'll have to take one of the all-night bars. Hey—want to join me?"

"No."

"Got your quota in, eh? Lucky. Every week I keep telling myself—"

Mohrlock lengthened his stride and left him behind. He

spent most of the night drinking himself into a state of sullen stupefaction. When his money ran out he staggered home and spent the remainder of the night in the chair in front of his window, looking out at the darkness. He heard Whitie getting up, heard him talking quietly with Mrs. Lynez while he ate his breakfast, heard him leave for the bakery. Uniform streaks of red heralded the contortions of a synthetic sunrise.

When he heard Mrs. Lynez stirring again, preparing his breakfast, he went to the kitchen. "I'm not hungry this morning," he announced.

She nodded indifferently and returned to her room at the rear of the house. He looked after her speculatively, studying her long, white Dalusian neck. When he realized what he was doing he staggered back to his own room, threw himself onto the bed, and sobbed brokenly.

VI

The week had passed, he had failed to make his quota, and for all that, life on the Third Level went its monotonous way. The B postman brought him an official envelope, but it contained only his allowance for the next week—six crisp ten-unit notes. He gave one of them to Mrs. Lynez for his room rent, and she gave him a receipt.

He did not know what he had expected, but to have nothing happen at all seemed ludicrous. Time passed, and his mood gradually changed to one of exaltation. He had fought a battle with himself and won. Never again would he flinch when he heard the word *quota*, or count the days of the week to calculate the time remaining in which to murder. The threat of an unspecified punishment held no terror for him. Why should it? The worst they could do would be to make him an A victim, and he considered that vastly preferable to the life of a B murderer. He had *won!*

His sudden upwelling of exuberance brought the return of his appetite, and he cancelled the cancellation of his breakfast. He talked with Mrs. Lynez, and even attempted unsuccessfully to coax a smile out of her. He went out for a stroll through town and a laugh at the first of the week quota snatchers.

And when, later in the day, he met Whitie on the street, he was able to answer his unasked question with a shake of his head and a smile on his face.

"Better let me buy you a drink," Whitie said.

"No," Mohrlock told him. "I'll buy you a drink."

"You really didn't—all right. Buy me a drink. And you can't say I didn't warn you."

Another official envelope arrived that evening, by special messenger. Mohrlock opened it with trembling fingers and jerked out a letter.

A form letter. Even Doctor Rudieb's circular signature was reproduced, and the two blanks were filled in with a clumsy scrawl. "According to my records your quota for the past week shows a deficiency of *ONE MURDER*. I am, accordingly, revising your quota for the present week only to *TWO MURDERS*. If your records are at variance with mine, kindly notify me immediately."

The letter slipped from Mohrlock's fingers. Whitie picked it up, glanced at it, and remarked, "Old Blue Nose must have been in a good mood today."

"I thought I'd won," Mohrlock muttered. "But I didn't. It wasn't a victory, it was just a postponement."

"How's that again?"

"Now it starts all over again. Five more days."

"Right. And if you want my advice, you'll get one of those murders out of the way—what's the matter? You look sick."

"I guess I don't feel so good."

"Better hit the sack. You didn't get much sleep last night."

Mohrlock shook his head. "I'm going uptown and get drunk."

That night he had his second nightmare. And the next night another, an illusion so realistic and horrifying that it left him with a morbid fear of sleep. For two nights he did not even return to his room. When Whitie finally tracked him down he was intoxicated, exhausted, untidy, unfed, and striking out with a belligerence inspired by terror at anyone who approached him.

He pointed a finger at Whitie. "Won't do it. Don't care about damned quotas. Don't care what they do with me. Just won't worry."

"Fine," Whitie said. "You're shaking like an advanced case of Deep Space Tremens. If you're not going to do it, and you don't care about the quota, and you won't worry, why are you trying to kill yourself?"

"Because I'm afraid I *will* do it," Mohrlock said and wept.

"It's the doc for you," Whitie said. "Come along."

The staggering Mohrlock followed meekly as far as the first intersection and then refused to go any further. "I don't walk down this block," he announced.

"Why not?" Whitie demanded.

"Guy works there I don't want to see."

"All right," Whitie said patiently. "We'll go around."

Eventually they reached the clinic in the Administration Building, and a B doctor gave Mohrlock an injection. He awoke in his own bed the following morning, very much alive but rather wishing that he wasn't. During the few hours that he was relatively sober he managed to write a letter to Doctor Rudieb, telling him precisely what he could do with his quota. When next he emerged from blankness it was the first day of the following week, Whitie had him at the clinic again, and there'd been another form letter from Doctor Rudieb. His revised quota for the current week was three murders.

"I know a B," Whitie said, "who sometimes picks up extra money by helping out with a quota. His robbery rates are reasonable, but I don't know what he'd charge for a murder, or if he'd do it. I could ask him."

"No."

"You should get a job. You need something to keep your mind occupied."

"Good idea," Mohrlock said. "What sort of job could I get where I wouldn't see any A's?"

"Well—"

"That's what I thought. The A's have done nothing to me, and I don't want to do anything to any of them. And I feel certain that I'm going to commit murder if I stay sober."

"That's what you're *required* to do!"

Mohrlock said grimly, "Did you ever imagine your fingers around one of those long Dalusian necks? If ever I get mine there just once, I'm lost. A man's entitled to a little moral integrity, even if he's a convicted criminal. My moral integrity demands that I never needlessly harm another human— whether it's by picking his pocket or taking his life. That first week I came awfully close to it. I shudder now just to think about it. I never want to come that close again, so I'm going to get as drunk as I can and stay that way. It takes some co-ordination to commit murder without a weapon, and I figure if I'm too drunk to walk I'll be too drunk to kill."

"It's your funeral."

"Better my funeral than one of the A's. Whitie, is it possible that deep down inside of every one of us there's an urge to murder?"

"I never felt it," Whitie said.

"Maybe that's because no one ever gave you a murder quota."

Even while Mohrlock was intoxicated the little Dalusian clerk continued to haunt him. He gradually developed a drunken obsession that the clerk was somehow to blame for his troubles. He went one day with a rock and threw it at the shop window. The window was not glass; the rock bounced back. He threw it again and again; it bounced again and again, until finally someone stopped him. Through all of it the little clerk stood in the window gazing blankly at passing pedes-trians and paying Mohrlock no attention whatsoever.

A fourth week came and went, with a revised quota of four murders. In a surge of drunken anger Mohrlock mailed the form letter back to Doctor Rudieb. On the days that followed he mailed his quota card, his book of report forms, and his identification card. When he had nothing more to send he sealed and mailed official envelopes. "My quota for the day," he would say proudly, depositing another empty envelope.

The other B's seemed uncertain as to whether Mohrlock was insanely drunk or a drunken lunatic. On the infrequent occasions when he was capable of thought on that subject, he felt positive that he was both. Even in his drunkenness he attempted to follow the little clerk home at night, but his pace was so unsteady, and he fell so frequently, that he was never able to overtake him.

Finally there was an interview with Doctor Rudieb, with Mohrlock seeing the doctor dimly through a cloud of alcohol, as from afar. The doctor shook his oversized nose sorrowfully and lamented the fact that he had given Mohrlock every chance and received no co-operation in return. Mohrlock squinted across the enormous distance that separated them and shouted vituperations. He left the room with a single word echoing and reechoing through the drink-fogged corridors of his warped consciousness: *reassignment.*

VII

"Man, oh man," the young cabin boy said. "You were really in orbit."

"Where am I now?"

The boy chuckled. "In space. Haven't you noticed the heat?"

"I notice it now," Mohrlock said.

"And that strap isn't to hold your pajamas up. You kept floating off your bunk. Here—drink this."

Mohrlock swallowed, shuddering. "What is it?"

"Beats me. You been having it every four hours since they brought you aboard. Don't you remember?"

"No. And I can't believe that I'd forget *that* taste in a hurry."

"Man, you were beyond tasting anything."

"Where are we going?"

"This ship only goes two places, and you're coming from one of them."

"I see. I think something was said about reassignment."

"I'd say you're doing real good if you remember that much. When they carried you in here I thought you was dead."

"I was," Mohrlock said earnestly. "That's exactly what I was —dead."

"Sure. And with a little luck you'll be sobered up by the time we make port."

On Daluse a Bureau of Criminology escort came aboard for him and whisked him away to the local headquarters, where he was kept waiting in an anteroom for more than an hour. His chair, after the twelve days in space, achieved a genuinely excruciating hardness.

Finally Doctor Fyloid summoned him. "Ah—Lieutenant Mohrlock." He beamed at him benignly. "Sit down, Lieutenant."

"If it's all the same with you, I'd rather stand."

The doctor's smile broadened. "Doctor Rudieb rendered a very complete report on you. I've been studying it."

"Generous of you, I'm sure," Mohrlock said, eying the smile uneasily. He had a lurking suspicion that Fyloid was a sadist who'd found the perfect profession for the indulgence of his crass impulses. The width of his smile probably indicated the severity of the punishment he was about to inflict. When he ordered an execution he'd have difficulty containing his hilarity.

"You seem to have been remarkably unco-operative on Bal," the doctor said. "Why?"

"Sometimes I have streaks of stubbornness," Mohrlock said absently. The medicine given him aboard the ship had a peculiar effect on him: his mind kept wandering. Or it would blank out unexpectedly and when he got a grip on it again he'd have time and people and places most perplexingly confused. He remembered Doctor Fyloid, of course, but in some strange way the criminologist reminded him of someone, reminded him of—yes, the little clerk on Bal! This struck him as a remarkable coincidence, because—except for their long necks—they did not look the least bit alike. The little clerk's face had expressed nothing at all. The doctor's face epitomized smug superiority.

"This is a triumphant moment for me," Doctor Fyloid was saying. He looked triumphant. "I am happy to inform you that you are cured."

"Cured?"

"The nature of your crime, the unusual violence with which you committed it, and your obvious conviction that the violence had been necessary, made us suspect that you possessed latent homicidal impulses. If true, there was a grave danger that you might yield to them again. The purpose of your confinement on Bal was, of course, to give you the opportunity to purge yourself of them. Doctor Rudieb feels that our diagnosis was in error, but my own conclusion is that you had the homicidal impulses and that you learned to contain them. I have your release papers here, and I shall sign them with pleasure."

"Release—you're turning me loose?"

"Certainly."

Mohrlock took a step toward the desk. "Bal—purged myself —contained—" He forced his mind to concentrate. "You mean the pickpockets and the robbers and all of the other Type B citizens on Bal are there to purge themselves?"

"That is correct."

"And you intend to keep them there until they refuse to— to—"

"Correct again. We have an obligation, not only to our own society, but to societies everywhere. We cannot release these convicted criminals to prey upon their fellow men. We must confine them until we are able to certify them cured, and we can't do that until they have learned to contain their anti-social impulses."

"That's monstrous!" Mohrlock exclaimed. "You give them a quota of crime, and threaten all kinds of dire consequences unless they fulfill it, and when they follow your orders then you say they haven't learned to contain their anti-social impulses!"

Doctor Fyloid smiled peacefully. "Are you attempting to

give *me* a lecture in criminology, Lieutenant?" He shuffled the papers on his desk and scribbled his signature. "There you are. Go out through that door, please. Doctor Laime is waiting to give you your hypnosis treatment. Nothing drastic, just a little memory blurring. Naturally we cannot allow the general public to become aware of the details of your cure, or our criminological technique would be rendered invalid."

Mohrlock ignored the papers. "The A's!" he exclaimed. "What are you trying to cure them of?"

"Ah! You are of course unaware that Daluse is the galaxy's most advanced center of robotics. It isn't widely known, but our achievements in that field are quite as distinguished as our work in criminology. It is only logical that we criminologists should make use of the Dalusian robotic technique."

"Robots," Mohrlock muttered.

"Precisely. Surely you don't imagine that we would permit our criminals to relieve their impulses on *humans*. Our unique criminological laboratory on Bal would be impossible without robotics. When our work is finally completed, Lieutenant, we confidently expect to banish crime from civilized society. Your own contribution, small as it is, should be a measure of tremendous satisfaction to you."

"Robots!" Mohrlock muttered again. "I went through weeks of hell to keep from murdering—robots!"

"Here are your papers, Lieutenant. Through that door, please."

Mohrlock's mind was playing him tricks again. The face that grinned leeringly into his was not Doctor Fyloid's, but that of the little clerk—a robot face. Its expression changed to one of astonishment as he leaned across the desk and tentatively gripped the alluring Dalusian neck. He did not really exert pressure until the little clerk began to struggle.

A robot.

He stepped back, finally, and the face toppled out of sight behind the desk. Mohrlock meekly picked up the papers and walked through the door Doctor Fyloid had indicated.

Another long-necked robot stepped forward to meet him

and took the papers. "I'm Doctor Laime," it announced. "If you would sit here, please—thank you—and watch the light—"

Mohrlock submitted resignedly. His next conscious awareness was of an entire room filled with excited, argumentative robots.

"But I had already begun!" shrieked the one that called itself Doctor Laime. "He may not remember."

"Remember what?" Mohrlock asked.

The Circle of Justice was as unreal as a half-forgotten nightmare. The tentacles of the Truth Detector entwined about Mohrlock menacingly. He met the Chief Jurist's gaze with a scowl. He remembered long necks like that, from somewhere. Robots, weren't they? Amazingly realistic robots. Produced by the most advanced robotics in the galaxy—and where had he heard that?

"Lieutenant John Mohrlock, did you terminate a human life by strangulation?"

"How's that again?" Mohrlock asked.

"You will answer the question, please. Did you terminate a human life by strangulation? Yes or no?"

"Certainly not!" Mohrlock exclaimed, making no effort to contain his indignation. The idea—all he did was push a robot around, and they were asking if he'd terminated a human life!

"Positive," the long-necked technician announced.

From the Witness Dais Doctor Laime squealed a protest. "He must have done it! No one else entered the room. But the hypnosis—"

"Nevertheless," the Chief Jurist said, "we cannot be certain, and Dalusian Justice must be certain. You know perfectly well that the law requires a positive record of an admission of guilt or a negative record of a denial of guilt. An exceedingly unusual case, I'm sure. *Dismissed.*"

Mohrlock walked thoughtfully out of the Arcade of Justice and moved his arms as if to embrace the sunlight. He had the idea that he ought to be elated, but instead he felt only a disturbing puzzlement.

He was free, and the court had returned to him a substantial sum of money that he didn't remember acquiring. That pleased him, but he felt worried not understanding what all the excitement had been about. A robot? With so many long-necked robots about everywhere, one less shouldn't have made that much difference. They acted as if it were a capital crime to put a robot out of commission. The jurists had been robots, too, which could have accounted for the fuss—but in that case, why had they turned him loose?

An hour later he was in a bar, having his fifth or perhaps his ninth drink and beginning to feel pleasantly relaxed, when his elbow was jostled by another blundering robot. Angrily Mohrlock flung his drink into the startled robot face and seized the long neck. Eventually other customers pulled him away, but not before the robot was wrecked beyond repair.

"Lieutenant John Mohrlock, did you terminate a human life by strangulation?"

"Certainly not!" Mohrlock snapped.

"Positive," the robot technician announced.

Another long-necked robot leaped to its feet, its arms gesticulating frantically. "Something is *wrong!* A dozen witnesses saw him do it. He had to be forcibly restrained. We *must* have this man for further study!"

"Doctor Laime," the Chief Jurist said icily, "you will kindly familiarize yourself with the law before you raise objections in my court. What you propose is ridiculous. Dalusian Criminology is the most advanced in the galaxy, as you should be well aware, and the Dalusian Truth Detector is infallible. The accused's denial is positive. *Dismissed.*"

A second time Mohrlock strolled from the Arcade of Justice into the sunlight. A long-necked robot crossed his path. Almost instinctively he veered off to follow it. He couldn't remember anything that gave him as much pleasure as he got from smashing these robots.

At the same time he had a dim awareness that he couldn't go on destroying expensive machinery indefinitely without being punished. The punishment didn't particularly worry him, though, because he already knew about that. They'd ship him off to a nice town where a lot of long-necked citizens lived— but of course *they* weren't robots, they were real people, so naturally he couldn't harm them.

The robot turned a corner, and Mohrlock quickened his pace to overtake it.

7

A SLIGHT CASE OF LIMBO

The wind's shrill moaning sank suddenly to a muted whisper, and above the clatter of rain on the corrugated roof George Cramer thought he heard a scream. He opened the door and peered doubtfully into the rain-lashed night.

At his feet the swollen river swished and gurgled around the pilings. The rowboat, swinging with the current, struck the side of the dock with loud, irregular thuds. Cramer aimed a flashlight at the distant shore, but the blackness casually swallowed up the beam. He could see nothing.

Suddenly the cry came again, a long, sobbing scream that hung convulsively over the river until a fresh surge of wind twisted it into silence. Cramer did not hesitate. He grabbed his oars and leaped into the boat, and seconds later he was headed out into the current, rowing frantically.

He shouted over his shoulder, but if there was an answering cry the wind wrenched it away from him. The chill, driving rain instantly drenched his head and clothing and left him shudderingly cold even as he panted and perspired at the oars. His erratic old heart filled his chest with its relentless pounding; his swollen arthritic hands brought gasps of pain to his clenched lips as he worked the oars. He shouted again as he turned the boat into the rampaging current and paused to flash his light. An answering call came from far down the river. Cramer bent his exhausted body to the oars and sent the boat rocking forward.

Long before he neared that struggling, helplessly bobbing figure in the water Cramer knew that he was dying, and that knowledge brought a half-smile to his taut face. It would be a good trade, he thought—his own feebleness and disease, his aged, worn-out life, for a young, healthy life with direction and purpose and meaning. Instead of a wretched end in the sordid loneliness of his cramped cabin, this unexpected twitch of destiny offered an embattled death that he could welcome and embrace fully. His sobs of pain were fervent hosannas as he drove the boat forward, punishing himself, struggling to focus his last flickers of life into one memorable conflagration.

And he reached his objective. A hand clutched the side of the boat. Cramer turned to assist, and at that instant his heart exploded.

He opened his eyes to the bare rafters of his cabin. An elongated patch of sunlight lay against the far wall. Beyond his window birds sang, and a light breeze caressed the trees overhead. He tried to move his arms, to sit up.

A voice came from far off, deep, softly soothing, pleasingly musical. "Easy! Easy! You need rest. Sleep . . . sleep . . . sleep."

Cramer slept.

When he awoke a man was bending over him. Cramer watched the round, placid face for a moment before he became aware of the dexterous fingers that applied a bandage to his chest.

"You're a doctor?" Cramer whispered.

"No," the voice sang. "No. I am not a doctor."

"A nurse, then." The idea seemed incongruous with this monstrous hulk of a man, but the fingers were infinitely gentle. "I was dying," Cramer said. "I died, and you . . . was it you—"

"Quiet!" the voice sang. "It was you, friend Cramer, who saved my life. And you need sleep . . . sleep . . ."

The next time Cramer awoke he was alone. He edged himself cautiously into a sitting position. The room was just as he'd left it when he dashed out into the storm, and that was —at least a couple of days ago, he thought, fingering his beard. But he felt fine. He felt wonderful until he moved his legs and his arthritis reminded him painfully that he hadn't been taking his medicine.

He hobbled over to the medicine cabinet for his pills, and then he decided to dress. His bandaged-swathed chest puzzled him. The strips of pink cloth were soft as the softest gauze, yet they resisted his tugging. He left them in place and pulled on his clothes. He eased himself into the chair outside his door and leaned back with his eyes closed to enjoy the sunshine.

"So you are up, friend Cramer!" the voice sang. "It is well. It is proper."

Cramer's nurse approached along a forest path, tremendous in height and bulk, walking with a rolling gait that made Cramer want to ask if he'd been a sailor. He stood looking down at Cramer, round face expressionless, eyes darkly solemn, a small tuft of hair ridiculously isolated on the top of his head.

But his voice was warmly musical. "How are you this morning, friend Cramer?"

"I feel fine. Just a little weak, yet. Thank you. May I ask who you are?"

"Who? You mean you would like to know my name. That is proper." He seemed to ponder the question. "Perhaps you would prefer to call me Joe?"

"Certainly, Joe," Cramer said.

"And now you are well. Now we shall remove the bandage."

The long fingers quickly opened Cramer's shirt and expertly unwound the encircling strips of cloth. The fingers paused as the bandage fell away. Joe's round face assumed a blank expression that Cramer could not interpret.

"You have not healed as quickly as I expected," he announced.

Cramer stared at the open incision below his heart. "You had to operate?"

"Yes, operate. You would call it that."

"Oh! You massaged my heart to get it going again."

"No," Joe said. "Your heart would not go again. It was a very bad heart."

"I don't understand."

"I'll show you. But first, the bandage."

Joe quickly bound the bandage into place and rocked away into the woods. Twenty minutes passed, a half hour, and he came rocking back. He carried a transparent, flasklike object, and he thrust it under Cramer's nose and then held it up to the light. "You see?" his voice sang. "A very bad heart."

Cramer stared incredulously. The flask did, unquestionably, contain a human heart.

"Very bad," Joe said again.

"You mean . . . my heart—"

"Yours. Certainly."

Cramer started to laugh. This Joe, he thought, was every bit the character he looked to be. "What's keeping me alive?" he asked, wiping his eyes. He pressed his hand to his chest, felt for his wrist, and stopped laughing. He had no heart beat, no pulse.

Joe said seriously, "But I gave you another."

"You said you weren't a doctor," Cramer protested.

"But the heart is no problem for a doctor! It is more . . . I think you would call it engineering."

"I suppose," Cramer said. "It's just a pump."

"That is correct. So I have given you another pump."

"A better one, I hope," Cramer said, feeling again for his pulse. He could not find it.

"Much better. This one does not wear out."

"All right. Whatever you did, I thank you. If this is a gag, as it has to be, I still thank you. Out there on the water I didn't much care whether I lived or not, but sitting here with the sun shining I'd just as soon stick around for a while. So I thank you."

"And I, friend Cramer, thank you. There is a bond between us, because we have saved each other's lives, but I think my debt greater than yours. I'll come again this evening."

He rocked away, carrying the flask.

Cramer's strength returned slowly. He knew that exercise would have helped him, but his arthritis seemed worse each day. The few hobbling steps he took about the cabin were searing torment.

Joe appeared punctually in the fading light of evening to songfully inquire as to his health and examine his chest, where the incision was healing in a neat scar line.

"I'll have to get into town," Cramer told him one evening.

"But why not?" Joe sang. "You are almost well."

Cramer lifted a swollen foot. "I can hardly walk. If I don't get more medicine quickly, I won't be able to walk at all."

"Myself, I do not go into this town. But if there is some other way I can help—"

"If you could get me as far as the Morton's farm, Ed or Ruth would take me into town."

"Do you wish to go now?"

"Tomorrow," Cramer said. "Tomorrow afternoon. The doctor isn't in his office in the morning."

"Tomorrow," Joe agreed.

He carried Cramer in his arms as easily as he might have carried a child and deposited him on the Mortons' front porch. He disappeared before Cramer had finished knocking. Ruth Morton drove Cramer to town and helped him hobble up the steps to the doctor's office.

Old Doc Franklin, who was some ten years younger than Cramer, examined Cramer's swollen feet and ankles with a puzzled frown. "I thought we had this controlled."

"So did I," Cramer said.

"But you insist on living out there in that damp hole."

"I ran out of pills."

"Let's see those hands again. Is it bothering you anywhere else?"

"My knees. My wrists, a little, and—"

"Elbows and shoulders," Doctor Franklin said. "In short, just about every joint in your body. Going without your pills for a few days wouldn't make it spread that quickly. Let's see those knees."

He took one look and tilted back to stare morosely at the ceiling. "I'll give you something different. We'll see what happens. I'd prefer to leave the shots as a last resort, but the way this thing is progressing that last resort isn't very far off. Now, then. Will you move into town where someone can look after you?"

Cramer shook his head. "Not now. Later, maybe."

"If you wait much longer you'll be totally disabled. Your choice will be between being moved by someone or starving to death. If you don't starve first, before anyone notices. For a supposedly intelligent man, and a retired college professor, you are the most pigheaded—"

Cramer listened with a grin. He'd heard this little sermon before—he heard it, in fact, every time he saw Doc.

"Stop smirking," the doctor said. "So you love fussing around the water. How much fussing will you do when you can't get out of bed?"

"I can still look at it."

The doctor snorted. "Anything else bothering you?"

Cramer spoke without thinking. "How about checking my heart?"

The doctor turned quickly. "Heart acting up, too? Darned if you aren't just a walking corpse." He reached for his stethoscope.

"Never mind," Cramer said hastily, pushing himself to his feet. "There's nothing wrong with my heart."

"There's plenty wrong with your heart. Unbutton your shirt."

"No. I never felt better in my life—except for this." He waved a swollen hand.

"Eighty per cent of the coronary victims say the same thing—just before they keel over. Unbutton your shirt."

Cramer picked up the prescription form and took two painful steps toward the door. "I'll give these pills a try. Many thanks, Doc."

"You," Doctor Franklin roared, "are stubborner than any jackass I've ever met, and I've met some choice specimens. Talk about spoiled children! Sadie Brian is bringing that brat of hers in this afternoon for a polio shot, and after seeing you I can look forward to it. You don't need pills, you need a good kick in the pants, and I have half a notion—"

Cramer closed the office door behind him and leaned against it, breathing heavily. A few more seconds in Doc's chair, and he'd have found himself attempting to explain a scar on his chest that assuredly had not been there the last time Doc examined him—and a heart that did not beat.

"Ready to go?" Ruth Morton asked.

"I certainly am," Cramer said.

Ruth left him on a bench in the sunshine while she got his prescription filled and did his shopping for him. They drove back to the Morton farm, and Ed took charge of getting Cramer and his supplies down to the cabin.

It was evening by the time Ed stowed away the last load. Dusk pointed long-fingered shadows out across the water. Cramer saw Ed off, and then he sat tilted back in his chair by the dock, waiting for Joe.

He came swinging out of the forest, his large face white, almost luminous in the growing darkness, his voice songful as always.

"So you have returned, friend Cramer. I was concerned for you."

Cramer nodded, wondering how to say what he had to say. He pointed at the sky, where one star winked timidly through the overcast. "You come from there, don't you?"

Joe hesitated. "Not there," he said finally and pointed at the horizon. "There. How did you know?"

"Lots of things. Your giving me a new heart. The fact that

you have too many fingers, which I noticed several days ago but didn't want to believe. And then—"

Joe held up a seven-fingered hand. "I would have said that you have too few fingers!"

"Why are you here?"

"To study, to collect specimens—"

"To prepare for an invasion?"

"Friend Cramer! Why would my people want your distant world? There are so many closer worlds, uninhabited worlds. No, I come only to study and to collect, and when I leave it may be that none of my people will ever come here again."

"I see. When you fixed my heart did you do anything else?"

"But I did not fix it! It could not be fixed. I had to give you a new pump, and other than that I added only a few things to your blood so the new pump could operate. Your blood was much too susceptible to what you call clotting. Now that will not happen."

"But if my blood won't clot, one small cut—"

"It will clot when that is necessary. It will do it better than before. But in the veins and arteries, and in the pump, it will not clot. Do you understand?"

"No, but I'll take your word for it. You know so much, and yet you say you aren't a doctor."

"I am not a doctor! The blood—that is merely chemistry. Engineering and chemistry I understand. But not medicine."

"It must be those things you added to my blood that made my arthritis worse."

"What is this arthritis?" Joe asked.

Cramer explained, exhibiting his swollen hands. "Maybe the new medicine will help," he said.

But the new pills did not help. The arthritis became an incessant torment that intensified daily. Cramer kept to his bed, moving his pain-wracked body as little as possible. Joe looked in on him frequently. His placid expression never changed, but his actions, his questions, betrayed a fumbling concern.

He was preparing for his departure. He had been on this world for a long time, he told Cramer. For many years, the way

Cramer measured time. His studies were completed; his collection lacked only some suitable specimens of larger animals. He asked Cramer's help, and Cramer talked with Ed Morton and gave him a wild tale about starting a new business. With Ed's help he began buying cattle, horses, sheep, hogs, goats, even exotic breeds of dogs and cats. Joe furnished whatever money was needed. Cramer wondered where he'd gotten it but thought it impolite to ask.

Joe put up a small corral for the animals, and he would take them away one or two at a time, leading or driving them down the forest path. After Cramer watched the twentieth cow disappear in that direction, he remarked, "You must have a large ship."

"Not very large," Joe replied complacently.

"Then how do you get them all into it?"

"That is only a small problem in packing," Joe said. And left with the first of an entire flock of sheep.

Joe opened cans and prepared Cramer's meals, and as the arthritis became worse he also helped him to eat. While he worked about the corner of the cabin Cramer called his kitchen, they talked.

"This arthritis," Joe said. "Such a thing does not occur among my people. I find no mention of it in my books."

Cramer nodded dully and managed to conceal his disappointment. Somehow he had hoped—he had confidently expected—that eventually Joe would be able to do something for him. A man who could casually supply a substitute heart and change the chemical makeup of one's blood should be able to handle a little thing like arthritis.

"I am sorry the things I added to your blood have done this to you," Joe said. "But I cannot help. I just do not understand this thing."

"Will it keep getting worse?"

"I do not know."

"With this new pump, and the new chemicals in my blood, how long can I expect to live?"

"Who can say? Life is a fragile flame that flickers in the

winds of chance. My own life would have ended in your river had you not generously saved me."

"Yes, yes," Cramer said impatiently. "But without accidents, how long will I live?"

"Without accidents, you will not die! You will not die at all. This pump does not wear out or stop."

Cramer stared silently at the ceiling, contemplating eternal life with eternal pain. "Could you remove the chemicals from my blood?" he asked finally.

"Perhaps. It would be difficult, and soon the new pump would not work. It would—"

"Clog up?" Cramer suggested.

"Yes."

"I don't suppose you could give me back my old heart."

"But that one would not work at all!"

Cramer lifted a hand, now puffed to twice its normal size. "Soon," he said, "perhaps as soon as tomorrow and certainly within a week, the pain will be so bad that I won't be able to move. I won't be able to do a thing for myself. Perhaps I won't even be able to sit up. I'll have to go into a nursing home and be waited on as long as I live. I haven't enough money for that."

"This money." Joe shrugged. "I can give you as much money as you wish to have."

"Even with enough money, can you imagine what kind of life that would be? Flat on my back and in agony every time I move a finger. And it would go on, and on, and on. Very few accidents happen in nursing homes. But it seems that I have no choice."

Joe said nothing.

"Only I do have a choice," Cramer went on. "I can have you put my old heart back, so an autopsy wouldn't stir up a fuss —they could think what they liked about the incision—and end things immediately, as should have happened that night on the river. Or I can take as much money as you can give me and go into a nursing home, where I would live indefinitely but helplessly in fairly comfortable torment. It isn't much of a choice, but it is a choice."

Joe waited politely, his large face a placid enigma.

"And," Cramer said, "I'll have to decide before you leave. When will that be?"

"I had thought—tomorrow. Tomorrow night. But since you have such a difficult choice to make, I could wait another day. Or two."

"If I can't decide by tomorrow," Cramer said dryly, "I won't be able to decide at all."

In the morning Joe carried him outside, and he sat cushioned by pillows and blankets and looked out at the river. Soon it would be summer, with the grating song of frogs at night, and leaping fish, and the sullen old turtle that always sunned itself on the big log a few yards upstream. He loved it all, and now, whatever he decided, it was lost to him.

If he entered a nursing home, perhaps medical science would eventually be able to do something for this synthetically intensified arthritis—or perhaps not. It would be a frightful gamble, because he would be doomed to endless pain if he lost. Lying helpless, closely watched in a nursing home, he would not even have the choice of taking his own life. The first time a doctor examined him there would be embarrassing questions about his heart. He would be a medical freak.

And yet—sitting there looking at the sun on the rippling water, any kind of life seemed good to him.

Until he attempted to move.

Joe came to prepare his lunch, maintaining a sympathetic silence. He came again at dusk to feed him for the last time—canned beans, canned hash, canned fruit, plenty of hot coffee, simple fare for a condemned man's last meal, Cramer thought wryly. He ate slowly, savoring each mouthful. When it was over Joe would deliver him to the Mortons with enough money to last him an eternity of lifetimes; or he would replace his new heart with the worn-out original and leave his body in the cabin to be found as chance might decide.

"Well, friend Cramer?" Joe asked, when he had finished eating.

"If I could use my hands," Cramer said, "I could flip a coin."

"I admire your courage, friend Cramer."

"I have no courage, Joe. Flipping a coin may be the only answer, because I haven't decided."

"If you'd like to wait another day—"

"That wouldn't help. If it were a question of *doing* something, I think I could choose easily. I had no trouble deciding that night on the river. But to sit here calmly in a chair and make a choice between living forever, even though in agony, and dying, is something I cannot do. So I'm going to leave the choice to you."

"To *me?*"

Cramer nodded.

For the first time Joe's round face registered a discernible emotion: shock. He staggered backward; his musical voice took on strident overtones. "Friend Cramer . . . *I* cannot make that kind of decision for you! You have no right to ask!"

"Every right," Cramer said calmly. "The whole business is your fault. If I hadn't saved your life, and then if you hadn't saved mine, there wouldn't be a problem. So it's up to you to decide. If *you* want to flip a coin, I won't mind."

Joe gazed down at him helplessly. A many-fingered gesture underscored his consternation. His attempt to speak produced only an inane sputter.

"I'm waiting," Cramer said.

"Very well." The once songful voice rasped hideously. "Very well. I shall decide for you—now."

He seized Cramer roughly, ignoring his gasps of pain, and rushed him into the forest.

Professor Zukoquol, Chairman of Gwarz University's Department of Exotic Zoology, watched in fascination as a foot-long statue of a sheep rode the conveyor through the Life Rehabilitator. A full-sized sheep staggered forth at the other end, baaing lustily. A twenty-inch cow followed, to emerge a slobbering, foul-smelling horned monster.

Professor Zukoquol's eyes gleamed with excitement. "An amazing collection!" he exclaimed. "Friend Joruloq, you have done a splendid piece of work. And you brought a full load?"

"Full to capacity," Joruloq said modestly.

"Splendid. You are to be heartily complimented. Except for your encounter with the human, of course. That disturbs me."

"It disturbs me, also," Joruloq said.

"Did he truly ask you to decide his destiny for him?"

"He truly did."

"Horrifying, is it not, that a supposedly civilized creature should have no developed sense of ethics?" Professor Zukoquol shuddered. "I should not have blamed you if you had smashed him on the spot."

"But that would have been deciding for him!" Joruloq protested.

"Or gone off and left him."

"That likewise would have been deciding for him!"

"True. This is why we sternly advise our fieldworkers to avoid contacts with intelligent beings. Their moralities are so unpredictable. All kinds of filthy dilemmas can result."

"I agree," Joruloq said. "Unfortunately I had no choice, because I was indebted to him."

"I'm almost inclined to believe it would have been best if he had not saved your life. But never mind. Since you had already allowed yourself to become involved, I must concede that you acted with commendable wisdom. Have you made inquiries at the medical school?"

"I did so at once."

"What did they say?"

"They promised to solve the mystery of the human's arthritis at the earliest opportunity. They do not anticipate any difficulties. He must await his turn, of course—they have so many high-priority projects on hand that it will be a thousand or two of his years before they can consider his problem."

"Generous of them to place him so far up on their schedule,

considering that the project would be of no importance whatsoever to anyone but him. What will you do with him in the
meantime?"

"Nothing."

"You do not intend to rehabilitate him?"

"Certainly not," Joruloq said. From a fold in his cloak he
took George Cramer—an eighteen-inch figure that stood in a
half-crouch with swollen hands upraised, a look of intense
surprise on his face. "No, indeed. I would not force him to live
in pain for a thousand or two of his years while waiting for the
medical school to find time for his case. I won't rehabilitate him
until they are ready for him."

You might loan him to the museum."

"I think not," Joruloq said. "I'd much prefer to keep him near
me. He did save my life, you know, and I feel both gratitude
and fondness for him. Also, he makes an excellent paper-
weight."

8

D.F.C.

A warm, sunny day in May, and a new job for me. I found the room in the basement of police headquarters—a big room, with the freshly stenciled letters D.F.C. on the door and an unholy conglomeration of transistors, coils and dials bulking large in one corner.

A bright young police cadet sat at a desk in the center of the room. These youngsters think a uniform is a license to play detective. "You're Jim Forsdon," he announced, before I could introduce myself. "The Old Man wants to see you."

I nodded and dumped my stuff into an empty locker.

The Old Man had his office in a cubbyhole off the main room. It was quite a comedown from the quarters he'd occupied upstairs as Chief of Detectives. He'd held onto that job past his retirement age. They were about to throw him out on his ear when D.F.C. came along, and he jumped at it. The Old Man was not the retiring type.

"Sit down, Forsdon," he said. "Welcome to the Department of Future Crime."

A glance from him could make a thirty-year veteran feel like a rookie. He had a lean, hard face, closely cropped white hair, and steely gray eyes that looked through a man, rather than at him. Small—five feet seven, one hundred forty pounds—you wondered how he'd ever got on the force until you saw his eyes. I'd never felt comfortable in his presence.

I sat down, and he asked, "Do you know what we have here, Forsdon?"

"Not exactly," I said.

"I don't either—exactly. The big boys upstairs think it's an expensive toy. It's up to us to make it important."

He packed his pipe, lit it, and then leaned back and let it go out. The department scuttlebutt had it that he bit through two pipe stems a day and used a pound of tobacco a year. "We have an invention," he went on, "which I don't pretend to understand. You saw the thing?"

"Anything larger than an aircar I don't usually overlook."

He grinned. "Walker calls it Cronus—for the Greek God of Time. It gives us random glances around the city on what looks like a large TV screen—random glances into the future!" he paused for dramatic effect, and I probably disappointed him. I already knew that much.

"The picture is hazy," he went on, "and sometimes we have a hell of a time figuring out the location of whatever it is we're looking at. We also have trouble pinpointing the time of an event. Eventually Walker will get the bugs worked out of it —we hope. Even in its present form the thing has a staggering potential. We've been in operation for three weeks, and already we've caught half a dozen holdups on that screen— *caught them before they happened!*"

"It should help us attain the ideal we've always worked for," I offered. "I mean, to prevent crime, rather than just catch the criminal."

"Ah!" he said, fussing with his pipe again. "Maybe I didn't make myself clear. Cronus gave us an advance look at half a dozen holdups, but we didn't prevent a single one. All we managed to do was catch the criminal a few minutes after he committed the crime. It raises an interesting question. Is it possible to change the future?"

"Why not?" I asked.

His pipe had gone out, but he kept puffing on it. "An interesting question. The problem isn't critical where holdups are concerned. The criminal is caught immediately, the loot is recovered, and the victim goes his way thinking kind thoughts about police efficiency. But what about murder? Apprehending the criminal ten minutes later won't help the victim." He took his pipe out of his mouth and scowled at it. "An interesting question. Now that we have our own full-time detective, maybe we'll find an answer. I want to introduce you to Walker. And Cronus."

Walker—Doctor Howard F. Walker—was hunched over his creation. There was no doubt about it being his baby, as you could see from the way his hands caressed the dials. He was a gangling-looking man, six feet one, maybe one hundred seventy pounds, forty years old. He had a long neck with an overly pronounced Adam's apple, and thinning hair. His face was gentle and dignified, and behind his thick glasses he looked like a very tired university professor.

He didn't hear us come up, and the Old Man waited quietly until he noticed us.

"This is Forsdon, our new detective," the Old Man said.

Walker hardly looked at me. "Cronus has something," he said. "If I can only find it again—"

He turned to his dials.

"That's one of our problems," the Old Man said. "Once we focus on a crime, it's sometimes hard to locate it again. The time interval between the present and the time the crime is committed naturally keeps getting less. It takes a different adjustment for each viewing."

His voice trailed away, and I watched the six-foot-square screen above Walker's head. Shadows flitted across it. A female shadow walking along the street holding a child shadow by the hand. Shadow aircars floating past jerkily. A row of male shadows grotesquely posed along a bar, their glasses making bright blotches. A room, and a female shadow moving around a table.

Walker bent forward tensely, sweat streaking his face, as he made delicate adjustments.

The scene kept shifting. A park with trees and lounging adults and running children. A room with people seated at a table—a reading room, perhaps a public library. A comfortable-looking living room with an old-fashioned fireplace and a bright blotch that was the fire. A bedroom and a female shadow dressing—or maybe undressing. And mind you, Cronus was no plaything for a Peeping Tom. The shadows were so shadowy that only their clothing gave them sex.

"That's it!" Walker exclaimed. He moved a motion picture camera into position and pressed a button. It whirred softly as we watched.

A nondescript living room. A female shadow opened the door and came quickly into the room. She threw up her hands and stood transfixed for a horrible moment or two. A male shadow bounded into the picture—a giant male shadow. As she turned to run he caught her from behind. His hand moved upward, and the knife he clutched glittered as he plunged it into her back. When he jerked it out it no longer glittered. He struck a second time and released her. As she crumpled to the floor he whirled, ran toward us, and disappeared from the screen. The camera ground on, recording the image of that motionless shadow on the floor.

Abruptly the scene changed. A restaurant with crowded tables and slow-moving robot servers. Walker swore softly and turned off the camera.

"That's all I got before," he said. "If I could come on it from a different angle, maybe we could locate the place."

"When?" the Old Man asked.

"Seven to twelve days."

It hit me, then, like a solid wallop on the jaw. I'd been watching a crime that hadn't happened yet.

"Plenty of time," the Old Man said. "Not much to go on, though." He turned to me. "What do you think?"

"We should be able to identify the man," I said. "He'll be

well over six foot—wouldn't surprise me if he were six eight or nine. He'll have the build of a male gorilla. And he limps slightly with his right foot."

"Not bad. Anything else?"

"It's an apartment or a hotel room. The number flashed on the door when the woman opened it, but I couldn't make it out. I'd guess an apartment. The scanner screen by the door means it's either relatively new or recently remodeled. The living room has a corner location, with windows on two adjoining sides. It's hard to say for certain, but I believe there's an old-fashioned sofa—one of those that have a back—along the far wall."

Walker slumped into a chair. "You make me feel better," he said. "I thought there was next to nothing to go on. But I saw it twice. How did you—"

"Now you know why I asked for Forsdon," the Old Man said, and I made noises intended to indicate modesty. "You only missed one thing."

"What's that?"

"Our assailant is left-handed. And don't forget that the limp may be something temporary. All right, Forsdon, it's all yours. Seven to twelve days, and you'd better plan on seven."

He went back to his office.

"Can you give me any idea at all as to the location?" I asked Walker.

"I can draw a circle on the map, but it's only about fifty-fifty that you'd find the place inside the circle."

"That's better than nothing."

"There is one thing," Walker said. "I'd like you to wear this. Everywhere."

He handed me a band of elastic with what looked like dark beads placed on it at intervals. "It's an arm band," he said. "Cronus picks up these beads as bright spots. I'll be able to identify you if you show up on the screen. We know it works, because the Old Man wears one. Cronus has picked him up twice."

I slipped it on and went to work with a map and a city directory. Walker was still perspiring in front of Cronus. He hadn't been able to focus on the crime a third time. The Old Man's door was closed, but his nasal voice could be heard bellowing into his telephone. When a technician delivered the developed film, I pulled curtains to darken one corner of the room and fed it into a projection machine.

I ran it ten times without coming up with anything new. I couldn't even decide whether the assailant was a chance prowler or someone known to the victim. No facial expressions. Finally I stopped the projector and made a sketch of the room from what I could make out in the way of furnishings.

The Old Man came barging out of his office, took a quick look at my sketch, and nodded approval. "We'll find the apartment," he said. "The sooner the better, I suppose, because the problem doesn't really begin until we do."

I couldn't see that, and I told him so. I figured the problem would be virtually solved if we found the apartment.

"You think it's possible to prevent this crime," he said. "I don't. Even if we find the location and identify the man and woman, the crime is still going to happen."

"Why?" I asked.

"Look at it this way. If we prevent the crime, it's not going to happen. Right?"

"Right."

"And if it's not going to happen, Cronus wouldn't have shown it to us—in which case we'd be doing nothing to prevent it, and it would happen anyway."

"That interesting question again," I suggested.

He nodded. "Whatever you see on that screen *will* happen, or you wouldn't see it. As far as Cronus is concerned, it already has happened. Preventing it is like trying to change the past."

"We can try," I said.

"We have a solemn duty to try. I have three teams of detectives waiting outside. Tell them what you want them to do."

I wanted an apartment living room with a corner location and a door scanner. That wasn't quite as bad as it sounded. The scanner was a new gadget at that time, and not many apartment buildings had it. There was always the chance of an individual having one installed on his own, but I could leave that as a last resort.

I put in a hectic day trudging through apartment buildings and squabbling with superintendents, and I found it the next morning—in a stubby little seven-story building on South Central. It was one of those apartment houses that went up when the city decided it couldn't afford the luxury of open spaces and opened part of old Central Park to apartment buildings. This one was a midget among the other buildings in that development, but it had been remodeled recently. It was equipped with scanner screens.

After the usual protests the superintendent showed me around. He let me into a rear apartment on the sixth floor, and I took one look at the place and caught my breath.

I pulled out my sketch, though I had it memorized by that time, and moved across the room to get the right angle. The sofa was there—and it *was* an old-fashioned job with a back. What had been a bright blotch in the picture turned out to be a mirror. A blur by the sofa was a low table. A chair was in the wrong place, but that could have been moved. What was I thinking about? It was *going* to be moved. Every detail checked.

"Stella Emerson," the superintendent said. "*Miss* Stella Emerson—I think. She never gave me no trouble. Something wrong?"

"Not a thing," I said. "I want some information from her."

"I dunno when she's home."

Her next-door neighbor did. I went back to headquarters and picked up the loose ends on the attempt to identify our assailant-to-be. No luck. And at six o'clock that evening I was having a cup of coffee with Miss Stella Emerson.

She was the sort of person it's always a pleasure to interview. Alert, understanding, co-operative—none of that petty, temperamental business about invasion of privacy. She was no young chick, either—twenty-six or twenty-seven, maybe five feet four, one hundred ten pounds. The pounds were well distributed, and she was darned nice looking.

She served the coffee on the low table by the sofa and sat back with her cup in her hand. "You wanted information?"

I fingered my own cup, but I didn't lift it. "I'd like to have you think carefully and see if you've ever known a man who matches this description. He's big, really big. Heavy-set. Maybe six feet eight or nine. He's left-handed. He might walk with a slight limp in his right foot."

She set her cup down with a bang. "Why, that sounds like Mike—Mike Gregory. I haven't seen him for years. Not since—"

I took a deep breath and wrote *Mike Gregory* in my notebook. "Where did you last see him?"

"On Mars. I was there for two years with Civil Service. Mike was a sort of general handyman around the Administration Building."

"Do you know where he is now?"

"As far as I know, he's still on Mars."

"I'd like to know everything you can tell me about Mike Gregory," I said. "May I take you to dinner?"

As my dad used to say, there's nothing like mixing business with pleasure.

She suggested the place—a strange little restaurant on the second sublevel of a nearby apartment building. There were lighted candles on the tables—I hadn't seen one in years. The waitresses wore odd costumes with handkerchiefs wrapped around their heads. An old man sat off in one corner scraping on a violin. It was almost weird.

But the food was good, and Stella Emerson was good company. Unfortunately, her mind was on Mike Gregory. "Is Mike in trouble?" she asked. "He always seemed like such a gentle, considerate person."

"Sometimes gentle considerate people change," I said, thinking of the shadowy stabbing that hadn't happened yet. "How well did you know him?"

"Not very well. I never saw him except at work. He stopped to talk with me now and then—that's all."

"Was he—interested in you?"

She blushed. I've never been a social reformer, and I've always more or less accepted things the way they are, including women. I've heard it said that the blush went out when women did away with their two-piece bathing suits and started wearing trunks like the men. I'm telling you—you can't have any idea about what's wrong with our scientific civilization until you've seen a girl blush by candlelight.

"I suppose he was," she said. "He kept asking me to go places with him. I felt sorry for him—he seemed such a grotesque person—but I didn't encourage him."

"You're certain about the limp?"

"Oh, yes. It was very noticeable."

"And about his being left-handed?"

She thought for a moment. "No. I'm not certain about that. He could have been, I suppose, but I don't think I ever noticed."

"Is there anything else you remember about him?"

She shook her head slowly. "Not much, I'm afraid. He was just a person who came through the office now and then. He had an unusual way of talking. He spoke very slowly, separating his words—just . . . like . . . this. Most of the girls laughed at him, and when they did he'd turn around and walk away without saying anything. And—oh, yes, sometimes he'd talk about California. I assumed that was where he was from, but I never found out anything about his personal life."

"But you didn't laugh at him?"

"No. I couldn't laugh at him. He was just too—pathetic."

"Have you heard from him since you came back?"

"He sent me a Christmas card once. He didn't know my address on Earth, so he sent it in care of the office on Mars. It didn't reach me until July!"

"Last July?"

"No. That must have been four years ago—two years after I left Mars."

I dropped Mike Gregory and tried to learn something about

Stella Emerson. She was twenty-eight. She'd worked for three years on Mars, and then she returned to Earth and got a job as private secretary with a small firm manufacturing plastic textiles. She made enough money for her own needs and was even able to save a little. She liked having a place of her own. She had a sister in Boston and an aunt in Newark, and they visited her occasionally. She led a quiet life, with books and visits to the art institutes. Her only hobby was photography.

It sounded wonderful to me. The quiet life. A detective gets enough excitement on the job. If he can't relax at home, he's going to be a blight on the mortality tables.

We were on our second cups of coffee, by then, and I motioned the old fiddler over to our table. "Miss Emerson is a very pretty girl, don't you think?" I asked him.

His bloodshot eyes peered at her out of a two-week growth of beard. "Yup. Shore is."

I slipped him a dollar bill. "How about playing us a melody that's just as pretty as Miss Emerson."

He gave her a clumsy serenade. She reacted just as I'd hoped she would. She blushed furiously, and kept right on blushing, and I just leaned back and enjoyed it.

I took her back to her apartment and said a friendly farewell at her door. We shook hands—yes, actually shook hands. In this day and age! And she didn't invite me to spend the night with her, which was just as refreshing.

I rode the elevator with chiming bells in my head and a wisp of the old man's music floating around them. I stepped out on the ground level, walked dreamily out the door, and hailed an aircab with my pocket signal.

And just as I was about to step aboard, it stabbed me like the flickering knife on the screen. In seven to twelve days—no, nearer five to ten days, now—she was going to be murdered.

"Something wrong?" the driver asked.

I flashed my credentials. "Police Headquarters," I said. "Use the emergency altitude."

Walker was crouched in front of Cronus, perspiring as usual

but looking infinitely more tired. "I haven't found it again," he said.

"That's all right. We can manage with what we have."

He frowned irritably. "It's important, confound it. This is only an experimental model, and it's maddeningly inefficient. With money and research facilities we could produce one that would really work, but we can't get that kind of support by predicting a few piddling holdups. But a murder, now—that'll make them take us seriously."

"Stop worrying about your blasted Cronus," I snapped. "What does that pile of junk matter when there's a girl's life to be saved?"

He blinked at me, not offended, just a very tired scientist trying to get his eyes focusing again so he could go back to work. "Yes, of course," he said mildly. "With a more efficient model perhaps we could save a lot of lives. As for this girl—if I can't get more information—"

"I've found the apartment," I told him, "and I've found the girl. The man was last heard of four years ago on Mars. Obviously he isn't there now, or Cronus is subject to hallucinations. We'll know by noon tomorrow."

I sent out a general I.R.U. on Mike Gregory and made arrangements to have investigators waiting on the doorsteps when Civil Service and Colonial Administration opened in the morning, and then I called the Old Man to give him my report. This is S.O.P. in any department he heads. He never pats backs until a case is closed. In the meantime, tell him anything at all and you always get the same question—"What have you done about it?" The man who doesn't have an answer soon finds himself working somewhere else.

Nothing more could be done that night, so I went home. I won't pretend that I slept.

Early the next morning we had a complete report from Colonial Administration on Michael Rolland Gregory. Fingerprints, photos, detailed description including the limp and the left-handedness, and the added information that he'd resigned his job on Mars eight months before and left immediately for

Earth on a Dawn Liner scheduled to land at San Francisco.

I got off an urgent message to San Francisco, and stewed around headquarters waiting for an answer until it was time to leave for another dinner date with Stella Emerson. And another handshake at her apartment door.

San Francisco did a thorough job, but it took time—two more days. Michael Rolland Gregory had hung around for a while, living in rundown rooming houses and holding a series of odd jobs. There'd been no trace of him in the past two months.

"He could be anywhere, by now," I told the Old Man.

"Including here in New York," the Old Man said dryly.

That night I found that Stella had moved the chair, not knowing that she was giving her apartment the one last touch it needed to be ready for her murder. I took her home after our dinner date, and in front of the door I ignored her hand. "Stella," I said, "I want you to know I like you a lot."

She blushed wonderfully. "I like you too, Jim."

"I'd like to ask you a favor—a very special favor."

Her blush deepened, with a hint of panic. "I'd like to, Jim. Because I—like you. But I can't. It's hard to explain, but I've always told myself that unless I marry a man—"

Her eyes widened in amazement while I leaned against the wall and laughed helplessly. Then I dispensed with the handshaking. She clung to me, and it might have been her first kiss.

"I don't just like you, darling," I said. "I love you. And that wasn't the favor I was going to ask. You said you have an aunt living in Newark. I want you to stay with her for a few days."

"But why?"

"Will you trust me? I can't tell you anything except that you're in danger here."

"You mean—from Mike?"

"I'm afraid so."

"It's hard to believe that Mike would want to harm me. But if you think it's important—"

"I do. Will you call your aunt now and make the arrangements? I'll take you there tonight."

She packed a bag, and I took her to Newark in an aircab. Her aunt was hospitable and co-operative, albeit a bit confused at the way I checked over her apartment. I was taking no chances that the aunt's living room could be the potential scene of the crime. It wasn't—no similarity at all.

"Promise me," I said, "that you won't go back to your apartment for any reason until I tell you it's all right."

"I promise. But I may need something."

"Make a list, and I'll have a policewoman pick up anything you need."

"All right."

I made her give me her key. I wasn't taking any chances on her making just one quick visit to her apartment and running into that date she was supposed to have with the future.

I arranged with the superintendent of her apartment house to have the lights in her apartment turned on each evening and turned off at an appropriate time. I put a stakeout on her apartment building and another on her aunt's. I got a detective assigned to tail her, though of course she didn't know it.

Then it was zero to five days, and I was quietly going nuts.

Zero to four days. I walked into the D.F.C. room, and Walker jumped to meet me. "I found it again!"

"Anything new?"

"No. Everything was the same—exactly the same."

"When?"

"Two to three days."

I sat down wearily and stared at Cronus. The screen was blank. "How did you happen to invent that thing?" I asked.

"I didn't really invent it. I discovered it. I was tinkering with a TV layout, and I changed some circuits and added new ones, just experimenting. The pictures I got were poor, but they didn't seem to be coming from any known station—or combination of stations, since they kept changing. That was interesting, so I kept working on it. Then one day the screen showed me a big aircar smashup. There were at least a dozen units involved, and I told myself, 'These Class D pictures are really overdoing it.' About a week later I opened my morning paper and found the same smashup on page one. It took a long time to get anybody interested, but finally—"

He broke off. The Old Man came charging out of his office waving both hands. "Brooklyn! Gregory was living in a rooming house in Brooklyn. He left three days ago."

The only good lead we'd turned up, and it led nowhere. No one knew where he'd gone. It proved that he was somewhere in the vicinity of New York City, but I don't think any of us had ever doubted that.

"One thing is interesting," the Old Man said. "He's using his own name. No reason why he shouldn't, of course—he's not a criminal. But he is a potential criminal, and *he doesn't know that.*"

I suddenly realized that we had a double problem. We had to protect Stella from Gregory, but we also had to protect Gregory from himself. If we could find him.

"Any suggestions?" I asked.

"Keep looking," the Old Man said.

"If we could only pick Gregory up and hold him for a couple of days, maybe we could beat this. We've protected Stella Emerson, we've locked up her apartment, and caging Gregory should close the case."

He laughed sarcastically. "You're still thinking we can prevent this murder. Listen. In one of those holdups we spotted, I recognized the crook. Butch Mackey—remember him? One leg shorter than the other, he couldn't disguise his walk in a blackout. I had him picked up, and he was carrying a gun, and we brought him in and charged him. He escaped, got another gun, and committed the holdup right on schedule. I'm telling you, the future according to Cronus can't be changed. I'm working as hard as anyone else to prevent this crime, but I know for a certainty that sometime today or tomorrow the girl and Gregory are going to meet in that apartment—or in one exactly like it."

"We're going to change the future this time," I said.

On my way out I stopped for a good look at Cronus. Nothing but a monster would give you a murderer, a victim, the place and the approximate time, and then leave you completely helpless to do anything about it. If Walker hadn't been there I'd have administered a firm kick to a vital part of its anatomy.

Walker called these two days the Critical Period. I agreed with him, except that he was thinking of Cronus' accuracy and I was thinking of the human life at stake. Stella's life. I called off our dinner date and prowled around Manhattan looking for a big man with a pronounced limp. One slightly grotesque speck of dust among millions of normal specks. It gave me some satisfaction to know that I wasn't alone in my search. Aircars were swooping in low for a quick look at pedestrians. Foot patrolmen were scrutinizing every passer-by. Detectives were making the rounds of rooming houses and hotels with photographs. Cab and bus drivers had been alerted.

For a man who had no reason to hide, Michael Rolland Gregory was doing an unbelievably expert job at keeping out of sight.

I radioed police headquarters at 10:00 P.M., and the Old Man's voice exploded at me. "Where the hell have you been? The stakeout at the girl's apartment nabbed Gregory. They're bringing him in."

I skipped the signing off formalities and ran. I tore down the corridor to the D.F.C. room and burst in on what might have been a funeral celebration. Walker sat with his face in his hands while the Old Man grimly paced a tight circle.

"He got away," the Old Man snarled. "Snapped the handcuffs like toothpicks, bowled over his escort, and made a clean break. The man must have the strength of a utility robot."

"How did they happen to pick him up?" I asked.

"He came strolling down the street and started into the apartment building. Completely innocent about the whole thing, of course. He didn't have any idea we were looking for him."

"He has an idea now," I said. "It's going to be great sport locating him again."

The Old Man already had a small army loose in the area where Gregory escaped, but for all they found he might have soaked into the ground. I called Stella and asked her to stay home from work the next day. I doubled the stakeout on her aunt's apartment.

And I was out at dawn, prowling the streets, riding with the air patrols, and I suppose generally making a nuisance of myself with calls to headquarters. We put in a miserable day, and Gregory could have been hiding on Mars for all the luck we had.

I had coffee for breakfast, coffee for lunch, and a fast evening meal at a little sandwich shop I passed while doing a foot patrol of the street in front of Stella's apartment building. The stakeout was on the job, and the superintendent had Stella's lights on. I stood for a moment in the building's doorway, watching the few pedestrians, and then I signaled an aircab.

"I'd like to ride around here a bit," I said.

"Sure thing," the driver said.

We crisscrossed back and forth above the streets, and I squinted at pedestrians and watched the thin traffic pattern. Fifteen minutes later we were back at the apartment building.

"Circle low around the building," I said.

"Oh, no you don't! Want me to lose my license? I can't go out of the air lanes."

"You can this time. Police."

He looked at my credentials. "Why don't you guys use your own vehicles?" he grumbled.

We floated downward. There was a narrow strip of lawn behind the building, with a couple of trees, and next to it a dimly lit alley. The cabbie handed me a pair of binoculars, and I strained my eyes at the sprawling shadows. I couldn't see anything suspicious, but I decided the alley might be worth a trip on foot.

The third time around I glanced at Stella's lighted windows —the rear ones—and gasped. A dark shadow clung to the side of the building, edging slowly along the ledge toward her window. Gregory.

The cabbie saw him at the same time. "The guy's *crazy!*" he exclaimed.

As we watched, Gregory got the window open and disappeared into the apartment.

I tried to radio the men on the stakeout but couldn't rouse them. I called headquarters.

"Forsdon," the girl purred. "Urgent message for you."

"Skip it!" I said. I snapped out a description of the situation and cut off.

"Can you move this thing close enough to get me through the window?" I asked the driver.

"I can try," he said. "But watch your step, fellow. It's a long way down."

He hovered close, and I grabbed the edge of the window and pulled myself through. Gregory faced me across the living room, a bewildered, panicky look on his large, childlike face. I was thinking, how stupid can we get? From the way he came into Cronus' picture we should have suspected something like this, but who would have thought that a man of Gregory's size could make like a human fly?

"All right, Gregory," I said. "You're under arrest."

Tears streaked his face. His jaw moved, his lips formed words, but no sound emerged. Suddenly I understood how we had blundered. This grotesquely oversized child meant no harm to anyone. Stella was the only person he'd ever known who treated him like a human being, and he wanted to see her again. For some reason he couldn't comprehend, the police were trying to prevent that. His entire circumscribed universe was mocking him, even Stella, and he was frightened.

And dangerous. He lunged at me like the utility robot the Old Man had mentioned and forced me back toward the open window. I got my gun out, and he just casually knocked it out of my hand. He had me on the window ledge, forcing me out, when the apartment door opened.

It was Stella.

"Run!" I shouted.

Then the night air was whistling past me, and from the window above came Stella's long, piercing scream. I crashed into the branches of a tree, struggled frantically for a hold, and fell through.

The doctor had a face like an owl. He bent over me, making funny clucking noises with his tongue, and when he saw that my eyes were open he grinned at me. "Not bad. Not bad at all."

"What's good about it?" I asked.

"Young man, you fell six stories and all you have is a broken leg and assorted bruises. You ask me what's good about it?"

"You wouldn't understand," I said.

Stella's scream rang in my ears. I twisted, and felt the heavy cast on my left leg, and my mood merged with the dull gray of the hospital room.

A nurse came tiptoeing in and smiled blandly when she saw I was awake. "You have visitors," she said. "Do you want to see them?"

I knew it was the Old Man. I hated to face him, but I said, "Let's get it over with."

He looked into the room, nodded, backed away. Then he came in, and ahead of him walked Stella. A different Stella— face pale and distorted, eyes registering shock and grief. But alive—very much alive.

I started to sit up, and the nurse placed a firm hand on each shoulder and made disapproving noises. The Old Man moved up a chair for Stella.

"Jim—" she said. Her voice broke.

"I'll tell him," the Old Man said. "It seems that Miss Emerson has a sister living in Boston."

"I know that," I said.

"A *twin* sister. The girl didn't know anything about our problem, and she came down this evening for a visit. She had a key to Miss Emerson's apartment, and she walked in just at the right time to play a role in Cronus' drama."

"Was she—"

"No. Thankfully, no. Her wounds are painful but superficial. She'll be all right."

I relaxed. "What happened to Gregory?"

"He tried to go out the way he came in, and there wasn't any tree to break his fall. One other thing—I have an urgent message for you from Walker."

I glanced at the slip of paper. "Jim, for God's sake, stay out of aircars!"

"Cronus showed us your fall half an hour before it happened," the Old Man said. "From our angle it looked as if you fell out of the aircab. Some time in the next twenty-four hours, Walker calculated, but we couldn't reach you. Why didn't you leave that damned radio on?"

"It wouldn't have made any difference," I said. "You know that."

"Yes. I know. Cronus can show us the future, but he can't change it, and neither can we."

"He changed mine," I said, looking at Stella.

The Old Man took the hint and left.

Five minutes later the phone rang, and I reached around Stella to answer it. It was Walker, and Stella held her face close to mine and listened.

"Just called to offer my congratulations," Walker said.

"Congratulations for what?"

"For your wedding. Cronus just picked it up."

I swore, but I kept it under my breath. "I haven't even asked the girl yet, and don't tell me I'm wearing that stupid arm band at my wedding, because I'm not."

"No, but you're on crutches. And the Old Man is there, and he's wearing his."

"All right," I said. "When is this happy event going to take place?"

"Four to eight days."

I slammed down the receiver and kissed Stella's blushing face. "Darling, Cronus says we're getting married in four to eight days, and this is one time that monstrosity's going to be wrong. We'll get married tomorrow."

"All right, Jim, if you want to. But—"

"But what?"

"This is May twenty-eighth, and if we get married tomorrow I won't be a June bride."

We were married five days later, and we went to Arizona on our honeymoon. I'd done some checking, and I knew Arizona was well outside of Cronus' range.

9

WINGS OF SONG

Karl Brandon saw the sign by accident. An aircar cut below
them, and he looked after it because it was a late-model
Smires, and his eye picked out one small sign of a row of small
signs on the roofs of the cluttered little shopping circle.

"Antiques," the sign said, and Brandon looked at his watch
and calculated that he had twenty-five minutes to spare. He
nudged his chauffeur and pointed at the sign.

Two minutes later he was inside the shop. He inventoried
the littered, dust-covered interior with one swift glance and
turned to leave. He had the patiently developed instinct of a
connoisseur, and his instinct told him there was nothing to be
gained by sifting over that shabby collection of junk.

The proprietor bobbed up at his elbow, a small, bald-headed
man who nodded, smiled, rubbed his hands together. "Yes,
sir?"

"Lighters?" Brandon said.

"Yes, sir. Certainly, sir. We have a fine collection, sir. If you
will step this way . . ."

Brandon propelled his bulky figure after the proprietor,
tromping the little man's heels in his excitement. He could always settle with his instinct later, and if this unlikely place

actually had a fine collection of lighters it would be the coup of his lifetime—here, in Pala City, right under Harry Morrison's nose! Morrison would raise an uproar that could be heard all the way to Arcturus, and Brandon would enjoy every decibel of it.

The proprietor placed a tray before him, and Brandon took a deep breath and looked the contents over slowly, savoring his disappointment. They were an unclassified mess of corroded, rusted fragments. There was not even a fair specimen in the lot.

"No!" Brandon snapped and turned away.

"Got one that actually works," the proprietor said. He picked up a misshapen piece of metal, thumbed it, and held up the flickering flame.

Brandon snorted. "My good man. I have seven hundred and sixty-one lighters in my collection, and *all* of them work."

The proprietor bobbed his head, yielding to the inevitable. "Something else?"

Brandon shook his head impatiently. As he reached for the door a second time he took a last glance about the room and hesitated. A strange object caught his eye, a strange object lying at the top of a heap of strange objects. Under the thick dust that covered its surface Brandon's sharp eyes caught a suggestion of luster, of peculiar texture.

He picked it up. It looked to be some kind of container with a long handle, but it had no opening except for two queerly shaped slots in the top and a jagged hole in the bottom that was obviously the result of a blow. Brandon fingered the hole, stared, moved the object closer to the light.

"What the devil!" he muttered.

Hovering at his elbow, the omnipresent proprietor emitted a triumphant chuckle. "Didn't think you'd recognize it," he said. "It's *wood.*"

"*Wood?*" Brandon bent over it for a closer look.

"Ever see any before?" the proprietor asked.

"I don't know. I think I saw a wood table once, in a museum."

"Possible," the proprietor said. "Possible. But it's rare. And this is a genuine antique. Look."

He held the object under the light and pointed. On the inside, dimly visible through one of the slots, was a faded label. "Jacob Raymann At Ye Bell House, Southmark, London, 1688."

"Genuine," the proprietor said. "Nearly a thousand years old."

"You don't say. And—it's made of wood?"

"Wood. From a tree." The proprietor produced a cloth and dusted the smooth surface. "From a tree," he said again, holding it up to the light. "Ever see a tree? Of course you haven't. There used to be lots of trees on Mother Earth, but they wouldn't grow anywhere else. Now there isn't anything on Mother Earth. The cost of war, my friend, is not measured in money, but in things irretrievably lost, such as trees."

"What is this thing, anyway?"

"It's a *violin*."

Brandon rubbed his finger over the surface. Beneath the luster was a delicate, wavy pattern, unlike anything he had ever seen.

"What's a violin?"

"A musical instrument."

"You don't say. How does it work?"

For the first time the little proprietor seemed unsure of himself. "Well, I don't know, exactly."

"Not much room in there for the mechanism," Brandon said, peering through the hole.

"My dear sir!" the proprietor exclaimed. "There was no mechanism in those days!"

"Then how the devil did it produce music?"

The proprietor shook his head.

Brandon firmly returned it to its place on the table. "What good is it now?"

"Think, my friend. Centuries before the last great war there was a tree growing on Earth, one of millions, perhaps, and this—this was part of its living tissue. A master craftsman shaped it with his own hands, for there were no machines in those days. It is made of wood, the rarest material in the galaxy, and it's a splendid ornament. Beautiful. For the wall, perhaps, or a table—"

"Ornament be damned! If I buy a musical instrument I want it to make music. I've made seven hundred and sixty-one lighters work, and I ought to be able to get music out of one antique —what'd you call it?"

"Violin."

"There should be books somewhere that would tell how it works."

The proprietor nodded. "Doubtless the University Library would have something."

"How much?"

"Ten thousand."

Brandon stared. "Ridiculous! It's smashed, it doesn't work, and there are probably all kinds of parts missing. Why, it's just a box!"

"Genuine antique," the proprietor purred. "Genuine wood. Nearly a thousand—"

"Good morning!"

Brandon let the heavy door slam behind him. His chauffeur leaped out and stood waiting for him. He stopped for a moment, lost in thought. It was time he developed another hobby. He was losing interest in lighters—there were no more good specimens to be had, at any price. And then, wood. Harry Morrison didn't have a sliver of wood in all his collections.

Brandon turned and re-entered the shop. "I'll take it," he said.

Morrison laid aside his magnifying glass and nodded gravely. "Yes," he said. He stroked a smooth cheek with long, carefully manicured fingers. The nails were tinted faintly azure. Brandon watched with a frown. He considered Morrison a bit of a fop.

"Yes," Morrison said again. "It just may be a find."

"That's what I thought," Brandon said.

"Or again—" Morrison tilted back his handsome, graying head and gazed at the ceiling. "—it may not. Let's see the picture. Ah—yes. It's clear enough, what you can see of it. Suppose this fellow is the musician that plays on it. Too bad he has the end tucked under his arm. Is this the best picture they could find?"

"It's the *only* picture they could find."

"Hmmm. Yes. Well, obviously there are pieces missing. These things—"

"Strings," Brandon said airily.

"They seem to run the whole length of it, though you can't see how they're fastened on because the fellow's arm is in the way. And what the devil is this in his other hand? Looks like a long rod."

"We don't know, exactly. It isn't mentioned in the description."

"Ah—the description. Let's hear it."

Brandon read: " 'Violin. The most important of the stringed instruments. Its main parts are the body, consisting of sound board, back and ribs; the finger board, which ends in the peg-box and scroll; the string holder or tailpiece; and the bridge. Inside the body is found the bass-bar and sound post. The four strings are tuned in fifths, g, d, a and e.' There may have been more. It was an old book, and some of the pages were missing."

Morrison looked doubtfully at the picture and shook his head. "Obviously there are pieces missing, and the description gives you no hint about the most important thing of all. How do you play the thing?"

"I don't know," Brandon said. "Even Professor Weltz didn't have the vaguest idea. He's going to study it. He took photographs and measurements, and he's having a copy made."

"Out of wood?" Morrison asked.

Brandon chuckled. "Metal or plastic. The professor thinks he'll be able to answer a lot of questions about ancient music when he figures out how to play it."

"Just what will you do with it?"

"Get it fixed," Brandon said confidently. "And learn to play it."

"That may be more of a problem than you think. Too bad there isn't a picture of one being played."

"Oh, we'll figure it out. What I wanted to ask you, though—" He turned the violin over and fingered the hole in the bottom. "The first problem will be getting this fixed. Who knows how to repair a hole in wood?"

Morrison was silent for a long time. Finally he said, "I'll have to make inquiries. Perhaps no one."

Brandon's private secretary was an earnest, hard-working young man who possessed a happy faculty for enthusiastically making Brandon's pet projects his own. Brandon appreciated this and paid him accordingly.

But on this occasion, as he carefully placed the plastic box on Brandon's desk, he did not seem enthused. He said glumly, "This is going to be harder than I thought."

Brandon opened the box for a fond look at the violin. "What's the trouble, Parker?"

"I talked to the Director of the Congressional Museum. They have one wood object there, a table."

"I remember," Brandon said.

"He said the table had to be repaired when they acquired it, but that was only a problem of finding an adhesive that would work on wood. They had all the parts—all they had to do was put them together. I got the formula for the adhesive."

Brandon nodded his approval.

"But he's never had the problem of supplying missing parts made of wood. He hadn't any idea how it should be done, or who could do it. I found a technician in our Polivar Division who thinks he could fit a piece of plastic into the hole—"

"Nonsense!" Brandon snapped.

"Exactly. He also thinks he might be able to do it with wood, but of course he hasn't any. He's willing to try if we'll furnish the wood."

"Get some wood for him, then."

"That's just it, sir. There isn't any. I've inquired everywhere."

"There must be some somewhere. I found this without even trying."

"It must have been a stroke of luck, sir, because everywhere I ask—"

"Yes. Trick is in knowing where to ask. Get me Morrison."

He waited impatiently until Morrison's serene countenance appeared on the wall screen. Morrison raised a hand in greeting —his fingernails on this day were tinted a dusky red—and said, "That violin of yours, I suppose."

Brandon nodded. "Harry, I'm sure you know every antique dealer worth knowing. Would you pass the word around that I want some wood?"

"I've already made inquiries," Morrison said. "If any turns up I'll let you know."

"Thanks."

"Unless it happens to be something worth saving. There's no point in destroying one valuable object just to repair another that's broken."

Brandon resisted an impulse to smile. His finding the violin had piqued Morrison more than he had realized. It went without saying that any valuable objects that turned up were destined for Morrison's collections. "No, that shouldn't be necessary," he said. "I just need a few small pieces."

"To be sure. If I find anything suitable, I'll see that you're notified."

Morrison languidly raised a hand and his image faded. Brandon twiddled his thumbs fretfully. He got up and paced the floor. He seated himself again, and his finger dug at a button on his desk. "Parker!" he roared. "Get me some wood!"

Parker dropped from sight for an entire week. He returned looking wan and tired, and Brandon, after a quick glance at his face, said, "No luck, eh? Where were you?"

"At the Congressional Reference Library, sir."

"You expected to find wood there?"

"Information about wood, sir. That's almost as rare as the

wood is, but I did find one thing. About a hundred years ago, on the planet Beloman—it's in the Partu Sector—there was a man who gave his occupation as *wood carver.*"

"I doubt that he's still available for consultation," Brandon said dryly.

"No, sir. But if his occupation was wood carver, he must have been doing something with wood—which means that he must have had some. If he worked at it very long he must have had a lot of wood, and there may be some left there."

"Wood carver," Brandon mused. "One who carves wood. One who makes things out of wood. But that's impossible! Even a hundred years ago there wasn't enough wood around for anyone to make a profession of using it. Where'd you get the information?"

"Out of a little book entitled *Strange Occupations.* All it said was, 'In the last census a man on Beloman gave his occupation as wood carver.' The Partu Sector is rather remote, and it may be that inquiries such as those Mr. Morrison is making wouldn't reach there. I think it worth investigating."

"Beloman. Sounds familiar. Do I have some interests there?"

"Yes, sir. You control some mining properties. If you asked your Resident Superintendent, I'm sure he could find out easily enough whether there's any wood available."

"It's an idea. It might even be a good idea. Have I ever been to Beloman, Parker?"

"Not to my knowledge, sir. Certainly not since I've been with you."

"I don't think I've even been in the Partu Sector. Parker, make up an inventory of my holdings in Partu and vicinity. It's time I made an inspection tour."

They landed on Beloman on a local Rainday. As they splashed their way toward a groundcar, Rozdel, Brandon's Resident Superintendent, sputtered apologies. "It's dratted politics," he said. "We get only one passenger liner a week, and we have one Rainday a week, and neither Intersteller Transport nor the Weather Control Board will make a change.

I keep telling them it gives visitors the wrong idea. I personally know of some tourists who took one look at this mess and left on the ship that brought them."

Brandon grunted noncommittally. Parker clutched the violin box close to him and hoped that it was waterproof. Rozdel got them seated and drove to a hotel.

An hour later Brandon pushed aside the mound of books and records and walked to the window. Beloman was almost a frontier planet, and there was a raw youthfulness about the city's broad, open-air streets and its orderly files of stubby stone buildings. Rain continued to lash against the window.

"Ever see any wood?" Brandon asked.

Rozdel shook his mind free from mining statistics. "Wood? What's that?"

Brandon concealed his disappointment. "If you don't know, there's no point in talking about it. See what you can find out, Parker, while I'm finishing up here." He turned back to Rozdel. "We understood that there was once a man on this planet who gave his occupation as wood carver. So we thought there might be some wood here. Now, about this depreciation schedule—"

"Wood carver?" Rozdel said blankly. "Oh. I remember, now. Old Thor Peterson calls himself a wood carver. I just never thought about it, but he makes knickknacks and things, and— sure. Out of wood. Charges fancy prices and works mostly to order. I guess he sends the stuff to Partu. People there may have money to waste on that kind of foolishness. They don't around here."

"He's still alive, then?"

"I haven't any idea. Haven't seen him—oh, for a couple of years, at least. Even then he was having trouble getting around. Pretty old, you know."

"I should say so!" Parker exclaimed. "Why, he must be—"

"Never mind," Brandon said. "If he's alive we'll go see him. If he's not we still want some wood. Where did he get his wood?"

"I haven't any idea," Rozdel said. "His relatives could prob-

ably tell you. I'll find out if he's still alive and get directions
for finding the Peterson Farm."

"Please do," Brandon said. "At once. Parker, order an aircar."

Beloman was an agriculture and mining planet, and they
flew over lovely, rolling farmland and crisscrossing roads that
were still maintained and used. There were occasional small
forests of giant darf weeds. Soon they crossed the boundary
into another weather zone and escaped from Beloman City's
Rainday into a luxury of golden sunlight. Brandon watched the
landscape impatiently. "Shouldn't be long, now. Isn't that the
river Rozdel mentioned?"

Parker consulted his map. "Should be. And that must be the
place just ahead of us."

They landed in a wide circle of old but meticulously maintained stone buildings—huge barns, storage sheds, a machine
shop, smaller structures housing clucking fowls or grunting
animals. The stone house, a tall, square building that had suffered the addition of wings on three sides, stood in the center
of the circle. They started to walk toward it. Suddenly Brandon
gripped Parker's arm.

"*What the devil!*"

It stood near the house, a straight, rough-textured finger
that pointed upward into a top-heavy crown of green foliage.

"Is it—"

Parker nodded. "A tree."

"I thought there wasn't a tree left in the galaxy!"

"Evidently," Parker said, "there's *one* left."

"Maybe he has more. So that's where he gets his wood.
Parker, that thing must be fifteen feet high!"

They moved toward it. The ground dropped away in a
gentle slope, and between the house and the outbuildings
were rows of stone-lined hollows.

"That's where he grows them," Brandon said. "Twenty-
three, twenty-four holes. But only one tree. Well—let's go talk
to the fellow."

They were met at the door by a plump young woman who

greeted them politely and led them down the slope to one of the smaller outbuildings.

"Go right on in," she said, and called, "Someone to see you, father."

They entered the building. It was empty except for a bench and racks of tools at the far end. A face turned toward them, old, grotesquely wrinkled, dark under a shock of white hair. The room was dim except for the brilliantly lighted workbench.

"Please excuse me. I cannot stand to greet you." The voice was old like the face—high-pitched and tremulous. "My legs no longer serve me," it went on. "My voice is almost gone. My eyes and hands are not what they were. Fortunately my appetite never fails me, and where there is appetite there is yet hope." He chuckled. "Your business, gentlemen?"

Brandon stepped forward and presented his card. The old man sat in a wheeled chair with brilliantly colored, coarsely woven robes tucked around him. On the bench lay a piece of wood; carved on it in bold relief was the partially completed head of a woman. Brandon gaped at it.

"You come a long way, Mr. Brandon," Peterson said. "Not just to see me, surely."

"We didn't expect to see you," Brandon said. "We—my secretary—found in an old book a reference to a wood carver here."

"How old a book?"

"It was published a hundred and four years ago," Parker said.

"Ah! Then it referred to my grandfather. Or perhaps to his father. We Petersons have been wood carvers for more generations than I could count. But I am the last. My sons have found loftier professions. My daughters have married farmers—good farmers. They prosper. And I, I squander what is left of my talent on trinkets because my hands are no longer steady."

"I saw the tree," Brandon said. "I thought trees grew only on Earth."

"Not even there," Peterson said. "Nothing grows there now.

But the Petersons have always grown trees because wood carvers must have wood. For a long time the growing of them was a family secret. When a tree was taken, there was always a new seedling ready for the pot. But no longer. I do not start new trees because I should not live long enough to use them. The one you saw is the last. When I have used it there will no longer be a wood carver on Beloman. But you did not come so far to listen to an old man's whining."

"That may be the last tree in the entire galaxy," Brandon said.

The old man sighed. "Perhaps it is. The growing is done with chemicals, and it is a laborious and painstaking process. I have willingly told the secret to many, but no one cares to bother. And why should anyone go to such trouble if there is no wood carver to use the wood?"

Brandon took the box from Parker, opened it, and placed it on the old man's lap. "This is why I am here," he said.

The white, deeply veined hands lifted out the violin, held it up to the light, turned it over and over. "Beautiful!" Peterson whispered, his eyes gleaming with excitement. "Beautiful! What is it?"

"A violin," Brandon said. "A musical instrument."

"Ah! They were real craftsmen in those days. They were real musicians, too." He beamed at Brandon. "I thank you for showing this to me. It is difficult for me to travel, but I should have gone far to see it. Beautiful!"

"I want you to fix it," Brandon said.

The smile faded. Peterson squinted at the hole, fingered it expertly. "Why?"

"Why?" Brandon stared at him. "It's broken. I want it fixed. Here, we have a picture of what it looked like. I want to learn to play it."

Slowly Peterson shook his head. With a final caress he returned the instrument to its box. "No," he said. "I'm sorry, but —no."

"But why not? Wood is your business, isn't it?"

"My grandfather had a musical instrument," Peterson said.

"A flute. He would go out into the fields to play. The animals would come listen to him. I saw them myself. He made beautiful music. Then he died. The flute became mine, and I tried to play it. I made some sounds, but I could not make music. The music died with the musician."

"What happened to the flute?" Brandon asked, with a sudden vision of an entire collection of rare and priceless musical instruments.

"I buried it. It was an old, old instrument—like this violin. The secret of making music passed from owner to owner until my grandfather could find no one who wished to learn. When he died its music died also. So is the music of this violin dead." He tapped the box gently. "Bury it," he said.

"Nonsense! It's a beautiful thing. You said so yourself. What's the harm in having it fixed, even if no one can play it?"

"Would you ask a doctor to heal a dead man? No. He could patch him, perhaps, but he could not heal. I would heal your violin gladly if I could make it speak again. But I cannot heal, so I will not patch. Bury it."

"I'll pay well," Brandon said. "You have the wood. You have the skill. It shouldn't take long."

"Too long," the cracked voice said. "Forever, and even then I could not heal it. But I would not expect you to understand. The music—the old music—was not like the music we have now. We have musical machines, and they are soulless. The old music—I know this, because I heard my grandfather play." He gave the violin a last, caressing glance and carefully closed the box. "I'm sorry you have come so far for nothing."

"Do you know of anyone else who could fix it?"

Peterson shook his head. "There is only me. Soon I shall die, and then there will be no one."

Brandon squared his shoulders, thrust his head forward, and said sternly, "I don't think you fully understand who I am. Even on this obscure little planet—"

"You are a man with a dead violin, and I cannot help you."

He handed the box to Parker, turned back to his bench, picked up a tool.

"Come on," Brandon said. He did not speak again until they reached Beloman City. Then he growled, "Conceited old fossil. I'll show him whether he's the only one."

On the glittering, cosmopolitan world of Partu, Brandon inspected factories, attended board meetings, made speeches, and bought wood. The indefatigable Parker scored one coup after another in tracking down owners of Thor Peterson's carvings—or those of his father, or grandfather, or of even more remote Petersons beyond number. There were wood boxes of all sizes, with carved lids. There were meticulously carved wood figurines. There were wall plaques, and sets of wood dishes, and carved serving bowls. There were even wood clocks that set in motion an entire parade of wood figures around their exteriors.

The list grew in length and variety. Brandon had no difficulty in acquiring the simpler items. Such things had always been for sale on Partu, and the Partusians naturally assumed that they always would be. Brandon bought, or graciously accepted gifts, and kept to himself his knowledge of the crippled old man and the one remaining tree.

The more elaborate objects, such as the clocks, were often family heirlooms, but Brandon had money, influence and the gift of persuasion, and he applied all three generously or ruthlessly, as the case required. In a matter of days he had the greatest collection of wood in the known galaxy, a collection that would turn Harry Morrison livid with envy. He had also, by promise of a nice bonus to Thor Peterson's agent on Partu, arranged to acquire the old man's entire future output.

"Now we can go home," he said jovially to Parker, "and fix this violin."

He sifted through his collection and reluctantly assented to the sacrifice of one small wood box. The Polivar technician took charge of it, disassembled it, and began to experiment, to learn to work with wood. He cut pieces, he pared them to the desired thickness, he shaped and glued them.

Days passed. Brandon contained his impatience and encouraged the man to take his time. He wanted nothing less than perfection on this job.

Finally the technician was ready. He searched Brandon's entire collection for the piece that best matched the delicate grain of the violin. He scraped it, raising a pile of shavings that Brandon contemplated sadly and ordered impounded. He could think of no use for them, but they were, undeniably, wood. With surgical precision the technician evened the splintered edges of the hole. With surgical precision he cut the patch and glued it into place.

It did not hold.

Brandon's disappointment was tempered by the arrival of a shipment of carvings from Peterson's agent on Partu: a small plaque, the one the old man had been working on when they visited him, and a pair of boxes with simple ornaments carved on the lids. Brandon inspected them critically and pronounced them inferior. He slapped his technician on the back. "He's second-best now," Brandon exulted. "Let's get on with it."

The technician tried a second time, and a third. Then, with ingenuity and patience, he secured the patch with braces on the inside of the instrument. It held. Gleefully Brandon called in one of his chemists and ordered him to duplicate the violin's glossy finish on the patch. The chemist grumblingly retired with fragments left over from the patching and began his own experiments. The task so tried his temper that he was even snarling at Brandon before it was over, but in the end he produced a finish not remotely unlike the original.

"Now," Brandon said, "we're getting somewhere."

Brandon and his technician studied the picture of the violin, and with the assistance of Professor Weltz they identified the bridge and the pegs. The technician carved them. They also identified the finger board, but Brandon was reluctant to sacrifice an object that could supply so large a piece of wood. The finger board was, Professor Weltz assured him, in no way functional, and its substance could not affect the instrument's sound. They compromised on one made of plastic.

The string holder posed a problem, since in the picture the violinist's arm hid that part of the instrument. The ingenious technician solved it by attaching a small bar around which the strings could be looped. The substance of the strings was the most perplexing riddle of all. Professor Weltz made an intensive study of the meaning of the word *string* down through the centuries, and he recommended the use of a certain type of fiber that Brandon had never heard of.

Brandon ordered the fiber—yards of it. The technician cut off lengths and attached them to the violin. Brandon extended a finger, cautiously plucked a string. The violin emitted a soft but recognizably musical *plunk*.

"We did it!" Brandon roared.

Professor Weltz demonstrated the use of the pegs to tune the strings. He showed Brandon how the placing of fingers on the finger board would alter the pitch. In a week Brandon could plunk his way through a simple tune and make it recognizable. In two weeks he had acquired a commendable facility.

"Now, about this rod the player holds in the other hand," Professor Weltz said.

"Hang the rod," Brandon told him. "I'm playing music. What more can you expect of a musical instrument?"

Morrison came, admired, and glumly departed with downcast shoulders after being conducted through Brandon's wood collection. The exultant Brandon waxed joyful for another week, and then a second shipment arrived from Partu. Cut in relief on one of the half-dozen carved boxes was a perfectly executed image of a violin.

"Damn the man!" Brandon muttered.

He envisioned old Thor Peterson bent over his workbench, producing this flawless carving from memory and smugly secure in the knowledge that he was the only man in the universe who could work with wood. Brandon sprang to his feet and paced restlessly about his office. He consulted his engagement calendar.

"I practically begged the man," Brandon growled. "And he said he wouldn't do it and no one else could."

He summoned Parker. "We're going to Beloman."

The usually imperturbable Parker was startled. *"Again?"*

"Make the arrangements," Brandon said. "I can leave day after tomorrow."

They flew out of the bedrenched Beloman City Rainday into the warming cheer of bright sunlight. With Brandon twisting restlessly and watching impatiently for landmarks, they passed over the rushing river and made a slow descent into the circle of farm buildings. Brandon leaped out, and Parker followed cautiously with the violin.

"The tree's gone," Parker said.

"He said he was about ready to use it," Brandon said.

They headed directly for the workshop, and Brandon had his hand on the door when a call stopped him. The young woman they had met on the first visit hurried toward them.

"What was it you wanted?" she asked.

"We'd like to see Mr. Peterson," Brandon said.

"I'm sorry. Father is dead. He died a month ago."

Brandon stared at her dumbly.

"I'm sorry," the woman said again.

"I'm sorry, too," Brandon said.

Slowly they walked back to the aircar. Slowly they flew away.

Brandon touched Parker's arm. "Let's set down somewhere. I want to think."

Parker landed in a rolling meadow near the shallow gorge of the river. Carrying the violin box, Brandon walked over and seated himself where he could look down at the gurgling, leaping water. The face of old Thor Peterson loomed before him in perfect clarity—the white hair, the deep wrinkles, the sunken, sadly meditative eyes.

"The music of this violin is dead."

Brandon opened the box and touched a string. Plunk.

"My grandfather had a musical instrument. A flute. He would go out into the fields to play. The animals would come listen to him."

Plunk.

"The music died with the musician."

Inside the violin, the faded label: "Jacob Raymann At Ye Bell House, Southmark, London, 1688." Nearly a thousand years. Centuries of great, stirring sound. Plunk.

In a sudden, intuitive vision Brandon heard music: heard a soaring, throbbing lament as a single, bewitching thread of melody was spun from nowhere with breath-taking, limpid sweetness; heard an incomprehensible blur of notes, a lightning rapidity of tonal movement, a darting, deadly, soulfully expressive rapier of glittering sound.

And saw an audience, audience of thousands, rapt, choked with emotion.

Plunk.

Brandon leaned out over the river and dropped the violin. He watched hypnotically as it spun downward. From somewhere nearby Parker cried out in horror, and Brandon ignored him. The violin struck with a faint splash, and to his amazement it floated. For a moment it bobbed lightly upon the rushing, tossing water. Then it plunged into a rapids, struck a rock, and another, and disappeared in a shower of spray and splinters.

Brandon turned away. Again he fancied that he heard music, but this time it was only the subdued murmur of the river below and the sibilant hiss of a hot wind searching the dry meadow grass.

Printed in the United Kingdom
by Lightning Source UK Ltd.
135735UK00001B/99/A